STORIES OF CHILDREN FROM DICKENS

Re-told by his Grand-Daughter
MARY ANGELA DICKENS

Illustrated by
HAROLD COPPING

ARCTURUS

ARCTURUS

This edition published in 2012 by Arcturus Publishing Limited
26/27 Bickels Yard, 151–153 Bermondsey Street,
London SE1 3HA

ISBN: 978-1-84858-868-4
AD002469EN

Printed in China

CONTENTS

"YOU SHALL BE OUR HEAD GARDENER WHEN WE'RE MARRIED"

STORIES OF CHILDREN
FROM DICKENS

BY
HIS GRAND-DAUGHTER
AND OTHERS

With an introduction by
PERCY FITZGERALD

Illustrated by
HAROLD COPPING

Edited by
Capt. Edric Vredenburg
10th London Regt.

RAPHAEL TUCK & SONS, LTD

LONDON · PARIS · NEW YORK ·

DESIGNED & PRINTED IN GREAT BRITAIN

LIST OF COLOURED PLATES

FROM
"LITTLE
PAUL
DOMBEY."

DICKENS' DREAM CHILDREN

By PERCY FITZGERALD

THE Reader of Dickens, be he child or man or woman, has this pleasing and yet unusual advantage, when he follows the tale of one of these dramatic fairy children, for he will learn that, in many cases, he is listening to the accounts of Dickens' own childhood.

In Copperfield, Boz, the name under which Dickens wrote, has taken so little trouble to disguise his revelations that in one instance I know of, he sent merely a family letter, unrevised, to the printer.

In Oliver Twist we find a suffering, agonised, drab childhood steeped in the horrors of the workhouse as it was then. The likeness of Oliver, as realised by Cruikshank, is strangely like certain portraits of the author.

It was Dickens who first thought of introducing an entirely new set of characters into his stories. What, it occurred to him, if he interpreted the minds and feelings of dogs, horses, birds, and above all, of children ? No one had done so before. It enlarged his dramatis personæ.

Whenever Boz comes to touch on the subject of children, a tender chord seems to be struck, charged with love and affection and all the sympathies. His very heart seemed to go out to them. This was owing to his interest in the poor crippled child of his sister, Mrs. Burnett, whom he framed, as it were, in that exquisite and truly perfect chrysolite, " A Christmas Carol," and where it is figured as Tiny Tim. All who heard the readings will recall his almost broken accents, as he described it ; and what a general flutter of joy there was when he officially announced that Tiny Tim did not die. I thought of Tiny Tim one night after a reading in St. James' Hall, when Dickens' son, then a delicate lad, who was lamed by an accident, was taken in charge by myself to bring home, and he had to be led carefully. It seemed an odd coincidence.

The master who contrived to carry off any awkward situation with a pleasant jest—for like Gratiano, his eye begat occasion for his tongue—we are told was a little taken aback, when it was first announced to him that he was a grandfather, and he did not exactly relish his patriarchal title. As the quivers began to overflow, he contrived a pleasant device for easing the situation. This was, he was to be styled affectionately " Old Venerables." It was a light farcical fiction which carried the thing off, and saved dignity and the suggestion of old age, which the children would naturally have accepted. Boz had no end of these little pleasantries. He was a boy, a child himself ever, and no one knew the child better.

Boz raised the engaging little world of children from the ranks to the dignity of most capable performers. He taught them to think and plan like grown folks, to feel acutely, show affection, and placed them on a complete level. Such seemed in the nature of prodigies, but such was his art that no one thought so.

He took us all into that wonderful fairyland which he created—where he made Lady Dedlock walk one night from London to Barnet and back, without fatigue, this miraculous feat being accepted as a matter of course simply because every one was delighted who cared to be thus amused. The engaging Little Nell or the ever interesting Little Dombey could never in real life have conducted any one so skilfully all about the country or have talked so wisely from morning till night. But what did it matter.

There were good reasons for the affectionate hold which Little Nell and Little Dombey have always had upon the reader. Boz was writing from experiences of his own, a family experience well known—the story of his affectionate regard for the sweet girl whose illness and death actually ran near to wrecking " Pickwick," and stopped its course for a time. This shows how acutely he felt her loss. He seemed to keep her memory green by reviving her image whenever he could. In a story introduced into " Nicholas Nickleby " she figured as one of "the three sisters of York ; " in " Oliver Twist " as Rose Maylie (the Scotch name will be noted) she also appears, not as dying, but not very far from it.

So with Little Dombey, who was drawn from a child of his own family, while, as we have said, Tiny Tim was the little Burnett, his sister's child. This touch of reality was sure to supply a strong leverage and motive force.

There is wonderful variety of patterns in the children he puts before us, but it is often difficult, particularly in the case of the lower class of his " boys," to settle accurately whether they are urchins, lads or youths. Boz himself seemed to be a little uncertain. In the case of " the Dodger " and his " pals," he himself would ·fluctuate, making the entertaining rascals now old, now young. They were called boys of say twelve years old, but at times the writer made them older, and indeed their talk is too wise and experienced to come from a juvenile. Boz had a rare delight in limning young rascals of this sort ; he renewed the pattern in Quilp's Boy.

The premier children—the " super-children," as Mr. Shaw would have it—in whose case Boz exercised all his power, and which rank in the very first place, were, of course, Little Nell and Little Dombey, also the pathetic little lame Tiny Tim. These portraits are of the most affecting kind, the reason perhaps being that they were drawn out of his own soul. Not only was Boz the introducer of these children, but he was also the creator of the most popular type—that is, of the heroic, tender-hearted, self-sacrificing, affectionate child, whom others, now that the way was shown, found it easy to make one of their characters—that is the advanced child, who was to a degree grown up. Nay, we go a little further still, and claim for him that he so elevated and purified the type that he brought this attractive form of child into real life and taught us how to love and appreciate it, which we did not before.

And yet these are, all the time, in Elia's happy words, Dream Children, lent from the beyond : spiritualised and yet accepted ; imperfect, as real as living. Alas, we do not meet, nor are we likely to meet, Little Nells or Paul Dombeys or Tiny Tims. They are true Dream Children.

TINY TIM

IT will surprise you all very much to hear that there was once a man who did not like Christmas. In fact, he had been heard on several occasions to use the word *humbug* with regard to it. His name was Scrooge, and he was a hard, sour-tempered man of business, intent only on saving and making money, and caring nothing for anyone. He paid the poor, hard-working clerk in his office as little as he could possibly get the work done for, and lived on as little as possible himself, alone in two dismal rooms. He was never merry or comfortable, or happy, and he hated other people to be so, and that was the reason why he hated Christmas, because people *will* be happy at Christmas, you know, if they possibly can, and like to have a little money to make themselves and others comfortable.

Well, it was Christmas Eve, a very cold and foggy one, and Mr. Scrooge, having given his poor clerk unwilling permission to spend Christmas Day at home, locked up his office and went home himself in a very bad temper, and with a cold in his head. After having taken some gruel as he sat over a miserable fire in his dismal room, he got into bed, and had some won-

derful and disagreeable dreams, to which we will leave him,
whilst we see how Tiny Tim, the son of his poor clerk, spent
Christmas Day.

The name of this clerk was Bob Crachit. He had a wife
and five other children besides Tim, who was a weak and delicate
little cripple, and for this reason was dearly loved by his father,
and the rest of the family ; not but what he was a dear little boy
too, gentle and patient and loving, with a sweet face of his own,
which no one could help looking at.

Whenever he could spare the time, it was Mr. Crachit's
delight to carry his little boy out on his shoulder to see the shops
and the people ; and to-day he had taken him to church for the
first time.

" Whatever has got your precious father, and your brother
Tiny Tim ! " exclaimed Mrs. Crachit ; " here's dinner all ready to
be dished up. I've never known him so late on Christmas Day

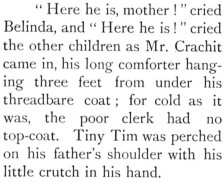

before."

" Here he is, mother ! " cried
Belinda, and " Here he is ! " cried
the other children as Mr. Crachit
came in, his long comforter hanging three feet from under his
threadbare coat ; for cold as it
was, the poor clerk had no
top-coat. Tiny Tim was perched
on his father's shoulder with his
little crutch in his hand.

" And how did Tim behave ? "
asked Mrs. Crachit.

" As good as gold and
better," replied the father. " I
think, wife, the child gets thoughtful, sitting at home so much.
He told me, coming home, that
he hoped the people in church

TINY TIM AND HIS FATHER

who saw he was a cripple, would be pleased to remember on Christmas Day Who it was who made the lame to walk."

" Bless his sweet heart !" said his mother in a trembling voice, and the father's voice trembled too, as he remarked, that " Tiny Tim was growing strong and hearty at last."

Dinner was waiting to be dished up. Mrs. Crachit proudly placed a goose upon the table. Belinda brought in the apple sauce, and Peter the mashed potatoes ; the other children set chairs, Tim's, as usual, close to his father's ; and Tim was so much excited that he rapped the table with his knife, and cried " Hurrah." After the goose came the pudding, with a great smell of steam, like washing-day, as it came out of the copper ; in it came, all a-blaze, with its sprig of holly in the middle, and was eaten to the last morsel. Then apples and oranges were set upon the table, and a shovelful of chestnuts on the fire, and Mr. Crachit served round some hot sweet stuff out of a jug as they closed round the fire, and said, " A Merry Christmas to us all, my dears, God bless us." " God bless us, every one," echoed Tiny Tim, and then they drank each other's health, and Mr. Scrooge's health, and told stories and sang songs,—Tim, who had a sweet little voice, singing very well indeed, a song about a child who was lost in the snow on Christmas Day.

Now I told you that Mr. Scrooge had some disagreeable and wonderful dreams on Christmas Eve, and so he had ; and in one of them he dreamt that a Christmas spirit showed him his clerk's home ; he saw them all gathered round the fire, and heard them drink his health, and Tiny Tim's song, and he took special note of Tiny Tim himself.

In his dreams that night Scrooge visited all sorts of places and saw all sorts of people, for different spirits came to him and led him about where they would, and presently he was taken again to his poor clerk's home. The mother was doing some needlework, seated by the table ; a tear dropped on it now and then, and she said, poor thing, that the work which was black, hurt her eyes. The children sat, sad and silent, about the room,

C

except Tiny Tim, who was not there. Upstairs the father, with his face hidden in his hands, sat beside a little bed, on which lay a tiny figure, white and still. "My little child, my pretty little child," he sobbed, as the tears fell through his fingers on to the floor. "Tiny Tim died because his father was too poor to give him what was necessary to make him well ; *you* kept him poor," said the dream-spirit to Mr. Scrooge. The father kissed the cold, little face on the bed, and went downstairs, where the sprays of holly still remained about the humble room ! and, taking his hat, went out, with a wistful glance at the little crutch, in the corner, as he shut the door. Mr. Scrooge saw all this, and many more things as strange and sad—the spirit took care of that ; but, wonderful to relate, he woke next morning feeling a different man —feeling as he had never felt in his life before.

" Why, I am as light as a feather, and as happy as an angel, and as merry as a schoolboy," he said to himself. " A merry Christmas to everybody ! A happy New Year to all the world." And a few minutes later he was ordering a turkey to be taken round to Tiny Tim's house, a turkey so large that the man who took it had to go in a cab.

Next morning poor Bob Crachit crept into the office a few minutes late, expecting to be roundly abused and scolded for it ; he soon found, however, that his master was a very different man to the one who had grudged him his Christmas holiday, for there was Scrooge telling him heartily he was going to raise his salary and asking quite affectionately after Tiny Tim ! " And mind you make up a good fire in your room before you set to work, Bob," he said, as he closed his own door.

Bob could hardly believe his eyes and ears, but it was all true, and more prosperous times came to his family, and happier, for Tiny Tim did not die—not a bit of it. Mr. Scrooge was a second father to him from that day ; he wanted for nothing, and grew up strong and hearty. Mr. Scrooge loved him, and well he might, for was it not Tiny Tim who had unconsciously, through the Christmas dream-spirit, touched his hard heart, and caused him to be a good and happy man.

JENNY WREN

WALKING into the city one holiday, a great many years ago, a gentleman ran up the steps of a tall house in the neighbourhood of St. Mary Axe. The lower windows were those of a counting-house, but the blinds, like those of the entire front of the house, were drawn down.

The gentleman knocked and rang several times before anyone came, but at last an old man opened the door. "What were you up to that you did not hear me?" said Mr. Fledgeby irritably.

"I was taking the air at the top of the house, sir," said the old man meekly, "it being a holiday. What might you please to want, sir?"

"Humph! Holiday indeed," grumbled his master, who was a toy merchant amongst other things. He then seated himself in the counting-house and gave the old man—a Jew, and Riah by name—directions as to the various business matters about which he had come to speak, and, as he rose to go, exclaimed—

"By-the-bye, how *do* you take the air? Do you stick your head out of a chimney-pot?"

"No, sir, I have made a little garden on the leads."

"Let's look at it," said Mr. Fledgeby.

"Sir, I have company there," returned Riah hesitating; "but will you please come up and see them?"

Mr. Fledgeby nodded, and, passing his master with a bow, the old man led the way up flight after flight of stairs, till they arrived at the house-top. Seated on a carpet, and leaning against a chimney-stack, were two girls bending over books. Some humble creepers were trained round the chimney-pots, and evergreens were placed round the roof, and a few more books, a basket of gaily coloured scraps and bits of tinsel, and another of common print stuff, lay near. One of the girls rose on seeing that Riah had brought a visitor, but the other remarked, "I'm the person of the house down-stairs, but I can't get up, whoever you are, because my back is bad, and my legs are queer."

"This is my master," said Riah, speaking to the two girls, "and this," he added, turning to Mr. Fledgeby, "is Miss Jenny Wren; she lives in this house, and is a clever little dressmaker for little people. Her friend Lizzie," continued Riah, introducing the second girl. "They are good girls, both, and as busy as they are good; in spare moments they come up here, and take to book learning."

"We are glad to come up here for rest, sir," said Lizzie, with a grateful look at the old Jew. "No one can tell the rest that this place is to us."

"Humph!" said Mr. Fledgeby, looking round, "Humph!" He was so much surprised that apparently he couldn't get beyond that word, and as he went down again the old chimney-pots in their black cowls seemed to turn round and look after him as if they were saying "Humph" too.

Lizzie, the elder of these two girls, was strong and handsome, but the little Jenny Wren, whom she so loved and protected, was small and deformed, though she had a beautiful little face, and the longest and loveliest golden hair in the world, which fell about her

like a cloak of shining curls, as though to hide the poor little misshapen figure. Old Riah, as well as Lizzie, was always kind and gentle to Jenny Wren, who called him her godfather. She had a father, who shared her poor little rooms, whom she called her child, for he was a bad, drunken, disreputable old man, and the poor girl had to care for him, and earn money to keep them both. She suffered a great deal, for the poor little bent back always ached sadly, and was often weary from incessant work, but it was only on rare occasions, when alone or with her friend Lizzie, who often brought her work and sat in Jenny's room, that the brave child ever complained of her hard lot. Sometimes the two girls, Jenny helping herself along with a crutch, would go and walk about the fashionable streets, in order to note how the grand folks were dressed. As they walked along, Jenny would tell her friend of the fancies she had when sitting alone at her work. " I imagine birds till I can hear them sing," she said one day, "and flowers till I can smell them. And oh ! the beautiful children that come to me in the early mornings. ! They are quite different to other children, not like me, never cold, or anxious, or tired or hungry, never any pain ; they come in numbers, in long bright slanting rows, all dressed in white, and with shiny heads. 'Who is this in pain ? ' they say, and they sweep around and about me, take me up in their arms, and I feel so light, and all the pain goes. I know when they are coming a long way off, by hearing them say, ' Who is this in pain ? ' and I answer, ' Oh, my blessed children, it's poor me ! have pity on me, and take me up and then the pain will go.' "

Lizzie sat stroking and brushing the beautiful hair, whilst the tired little dressmaker leant against her when they were at home again, and as she kissed her good-night, a miserable old man stumbled into the room. " How's my Jenny Wren, best of children ? " he mumbled, as he shuffled unsteadily towards her, but Jenny pointed her small finger towards him exclaiming—" Go along with you, you bad, wicked, old child, you troublesome, wicked, old thing, I know where you have been, I know your tricks and your manners." The wretched man began to whimper, like a scolded child. "Slave, slave, slave, from morning to night," went on Jenny, still shaking her finger at him, " and all for this ; ain't you ashamed of yourself, you disgraceful boy ? "

" Yes ; my dear, yes," stammered the tipsy old father,

tumbling into a corner. Thus was the poor little dolls' dress-maker dragged down day by day by the very hands that should have cared for and held her up ; poor, poor little dolls' dress-maker !

One day when Jenny was on her way home with Riah, who had accompanied her on one of her expeditions to the West End, they came on a small crowd of people. A tipsy man had been knocked down and badly hurt.

"Let us see what it is !" said Jenny, coming swiftly forward on her crutches. The next moment she exclaimed—"Oh, gentle-men—gentlemen, he is my child, he belongs to me, my poor, bad old child ! "

"Your child—belongs to you," repeated the man who was about to lift the helpless figure on to a stretcher, which had been brought for the purpose.

"Aye, it's old Dolls—tipsy old Dolls," cried some one in the crowd, for it was by this name that they knew the old man.

" He's her father, sir," said Riah in a low tone to the doctor, who was now bending over the stretcher.

"So much the worse," answered the doctor, " for the man is dead."

Yes, "Mr. Dolls" was dead, and many were the dresses which the weary fingers of the sorrowful little worker must make in order to pay for his humble funeral, and buy a black frock for herself. Riah sat by her in her poor room, saying a word of comfort now and then, and Lizzie came and went, and did all manner of little things to help her ; but often the tears rolled down on to her work.

"My poor child," she said to Riah, "my poor old child, and to think I scolded him so."

"You were always a good, brave, patient girl," returned Riah, smiling a little over her quaint fancy about her *child*, "always good and patient, however tired."

And so the poor little "person of the house" was left alone

but for the faithful affection of the kind Jew, and her friend
Lizzie, but her room grew pretty and comfortable, for she was in
great request in her "profession," as she called it, and there was
now no one to spend and waste her earnings.

SMIKE, AND DOTHEBOYS HALL

THE story of poor Smike is told in that wonderful book 'Nicholas Nickleby.'

Nicholas first met Smike at a school in Yorkshire called Dotheboys Hall, kept by a Mr. Squeers. It was a wretched, miserable place this Dotheboys Hall; Squeers was a hard, wicked man, and Mrs. Squeers was nearly as bad. The first time we hear of Squeers he was in London at "The Saracen's Head," where he occasionally went to bring down new boys, and he was speaking very cruelly to a new little boy, when, just then, a waiter said someone wished to see him. Instantly Squeers changed his manner, and pretending he did not know anyone was coming said,

" My dear child, all people have their trials. This early trial of yours that is fit to make your little heart burst, and your very eyes to come out of your head with crying, what is it ? Nothing ; less than nothing. You are leaving your friends, but you will have a father in me, my dear, and a mother in Mrs. Squeers. At the delightful village of Dotheboys, near Greta Bridge, in Yorkshire, where youths are boarded, clothed, booked, washed, furnished with pocket money, and provided with all necessaries." But really the boys were half-starved and neglected, and taught nothing, and the most wretched and miserable of all was the poor boy Smike.

Smike had never known a father or a mother. He was beaten and ill-used every day of his unhappy life, and until Nicholas came to Dotheboys Hall, as assistant master, had never known a kind word.

We ought all to be very glad that our schools to-day are not like that terrible place. You can imagine Nicholas's surprise when Mr. Squeers took his class the day after the arrival of the new master.

Obedient to Mr. Squeers' summons there ranged themselves in front of the schoolmaster's desk half-a-dozen scarecrows, out at knees and elbows, one of whom placed a torn and filthy book beneath his learned eye.

" This is the first class in English spelling and philosophy, Nickleby," said Squeers, beckoning to Nicholas to stand beside him. " We'll get up a Latin one, and hand that over to you. Now, then, where's the first boy ? "

" Please, sir, he's cleaning the back parlour window," said the temporary head of the philosophical class.

" So he is, to be sure," rejoined Squeers. " We go upon the practical mode of teaching, Nickleby ; the regular education system. C-l-e-a-n, clean, verb active, to make bright, to scour. W-i-n, win, d-e-r, der, winder a casement. When the boy knows this out of a book he goes and does it. It's just the same principle as the use of the globes. Where's the second boy ? "

" Please, sir, he's weeding the garden," replied a small voice.

"To be sure," said Squeers, by no means disconcerted. "So he is. B-o-t, bot, t-i-n, tin, bottin, n-e-y, ney, bottinney, noun substantive, a knowledge of plants. When he has learned that bottinney means a knowledge of plants he goes and knows 'em. That's our system, Nickleby. What do you think of it?"

"It's a very useful one, at any rate," answered Nicholas significantly.

"I believe you," rejoined Squeers, not remarking the emphasis of his usher. "Third boy, what's a horse?"

"A beast, sir," replied the boy.

"So it is," said Squeers. "Ain't it, Nickleby?"

"I believe there is no doubt of that, sir," answered Nicholas.

"Of course there isn't," said Squeers. "A horse is a quadruped, and quadruped's Latin for beast, as everybody that's gone through the grammar knows, or else where's the use of having grammars at all?"

"Where, indeed!" said Nicholas abstractedly.

"As you're perfect in that," resumed Squeers, turning to the boy, "go and look after *my* horse, and rub him down well, or I'll rub you down. The rest of the class go and draw water up till somebody tells you to leave off, for it's washing day to-morrow, and they want the coppers filled."

So saying he dismissed the first class to their experiments in practical philosophy, and eyed Nicholas with a look half cunning and half doubtful, as if he were not altogether certain what he might think of him by this time.

"That's the way we do it, Nickleby," he said after a long pause.

Nicholas shrugged his shoulders in a manner that was scarcely perceptible, and said he saw it was.

"And a very good way it is, too," said Squeers. "Now, just take those fourteen little boys and hear them some reading, because you know you must begin to be useful, and idling about here won't do."

You can quite understand how astonished Nicholas was at all

this, for it showed that Mr. Squeers was not only a coarse, common man, but that he could not even spell the most simple words. Nicholas, when school was over, was thinking deeply about the place he had come to, when he all at once encountered the upturned face of Smike, who was on his knees before the stove, picking up a few stray cinders from the hearth and planting them on the fire. He had paused to steal a look at Nicholas, and when he saw that he was observed shrunk back as if expecting a blow.

"You need not fear me," said Nicholas, kindly. "Are you cold ? "

" N-n-o."

" You are shivering."

" I am not cold," replied Smike, quickly. " I am used to it."

There was such an obvious fear of giving offence in his manner, and he was such a timid, broken-spirited creature, that Nicholas could not help exclaiming, " Poor fellow ! "

If he had struck the drudge he would have slunk away without a word. But now he burst into tears.

" Oh dear, oh dear ! " he cried, covering his face with his cracked and horny hands. " My heart will break. It will, it will."

" Hush ! " said Nicholas, laying his hand upon his shoulder. " Be a man ; you are nearly one by years."

" By years ! " cried Smike. " Oh dear, dear, how many of them ! How many of them since I was a little child, younger than any that are here now ! Where are they all ? "

" Whom do you speak of ? " inquired Nicholas, wishing to rouse the poor half-witted creature to reason. " Tell me."

" My friends," he replied, " myself—my—oh ! what sufferings mine have been ! "

" There is always hope," said Nicholas ; he knew not what to say.

" No," rejoined the other ; " no, none for me. Do you remember the boy that died here ? "

"I was not here, you know," said Nicholas, gently. "But what of him?"

"Why," replied the youth, drawing closer to his questioner's side, "I was with him at night, and when it was all silent he cried no more for friends he wished to come and sit with him, but began to see faces round his bed that came from home; he said they smiled, and talked to him; and he died at last lifting his head to kiss them. Do you hear?"

"Yes, yes," replied Nicholas.

"What faces will smile on me when I die?" said his companion, shivering. "Who will talk to me in those long nights? They cannot come from home; they would frighten me if they did, for I don't know what it is, and shouldn't know them. Pain and fear, pain and fear for me, alive or dead. No hope, no hope!" The bell rang for bed, and the boy subsiding at the sound into his usual listless state, crept away as if anxious to avoid notice.

After this Nicholas showed what kindness he could to poor Smike, but his doing so made things even worse for the unhappy lad. Mr. and Mrs. Squeers were more cruel to him than ever. After a while, when Nicholas had made up his mind to leave

Dotheboys Hall, one day he found Smike poring over a tattered book, with the traces of recent tears still upon his face, trying hard to do his lessons.

The poor soul was vainly endeavouring to master a task which some child of nine years old, possessed of ordinary powers, could have conquered with ease, but which to the addled brain of the crushed boy of nineteen was a sealed and hopeless mystery. Yet there he sat, patiently conning the page again and again, stimulated by no boyish ambition, for he was the common jest and scoff even of the uncouth objects that congregated about him, but inspired by the one eager desire to please his solitary friend.

Nicholas laid his hand upon his shoulder.

"I can't do it," said the dejected creature, looking up with bitter disappointment in every feature. "No, no."

"Do not try," replied Nicholas. The boy shook his head, and, closing the book with a sigh, looked vacantly round, and laid his head upon his arm. He was weeping. "Do not," said Nicholas, in an agitated voice; "I cannot bear to see you."

"They are more hard with me than ever," sobbed the boy.

"I know it," rejoined Nicholas. "They are."

"But for you," said the outcast, "I should die. They would kill me; they would, I know they would."

"You will do better, poor fellow," replied Nicholas, shaking his head mournfully, "when I am gone."

"Gone!" cried the other, looking intently in his face.

"Softly," rejoined Nicholas. "Yes."

"Are you going?" demanded the boy in an earnest whisper.

"I cannot say," replied Nicholas; "I was speaking more to my own thoughts than to you."

"Tell me," said the boy imploringly. "Oh, do tell me; _will_ you go—_will_ you?"

"I shall be driven to that at last!" said Nicholas. "The world is before me, after all."

"Tell me," urged Smike, "is the world as bad and dismal as this place?"

"Heaven forbid," replied Nicholas, pursuing the train of his own thoughts; "its hardest, coarsest toil were happiness to this."

"Should I ever meet you there?" demanded the boy, speaking with unusual wildness and volubility.

"Yes," replied Nicholas, willing to soothe him.

"No, no!" said the other, clasping him by the hand. "Should I—should I—tell me that again. Say I should be sure to find you."

"You would," replied Nicholas, with the same humane intention, "and I would help and aid you, and not bring fresh sorrow on you as I have done here."

The boy caught both the young man's hands passionately in his, and hugging them to his breast uttered a few broken sounds, which were unintelligible. Squeers entered at the moment, and he shrunk back into his old corner.

Well, the very next day Smike disappeared. He knew Nicholas was going to leave the school, so the poor lad ran away, hoping some day to meet the only person in the world who had been kind to him.

Mr. Squeers was furious. He hunted high and low, but could not find the runaway. Then Mrs. Squeers set off in the pony and trap to search the country, and a day or two later she found and brought home poor Smike, looking more dead than alive.

The news that Smike had been caught and brought back in triumph ran like wildfire through the hungry community, and expectation was on tiptoe all the morning. On tiptoe it was destined to remain, however, until the afternoon, when Squeers, having refreshed himself with his dinner, with a countenance of portentous import and a fearful instrument of flagellation, strong, supple, wax-ended and new—in short, purchased that morning expressly for the occasion, asked, in a tremendous voice, "Is every boy here?"

Every boy was there, but every boy was afraid to speak; so Squeers glared along the lines to assure himself, and every eye drooped and every head cowered down as he did so.

"Each boy keep his place," said Squeers, administering his favourite blow to the desk, and regarding with gloomy satisfaction the universal start which it never failed to occasion. "Nickleby, to your desk, sir."

It was remarked by more than one small observer that there was a very curious and unusual expression on the usher's face, but he took his seat without opening his lips in reply; and Squeers, casting a triumphant glance at his assistant and a look of most comprehensive despotism on the boys, left the room, and shortly afterwards returned, dragging Smike by the collar—or rather by that fragment of his jacket which was nearest the place where his collar would have been had he boasted such a decoration.

In any other place the appearance of the wretched, jaded, spiritless object would have occasioned a murmur of compassion and remonstrance. It had some effect even there; for the lookers-on moved uneasily in their seats, and a few of the boldest ventured to steal looks at each other, expressive of indignation and pity.

They were lost on Squeers, however, whose gaze was fastened on the luckless Smike as he inquired, according to custom in such cases, whether he had anything to say for himself.

"Nothing, I suppose?" said Squeers, with a diabolical grin.

Smike glanced round, and his eye rested for an instant on Nicholas, as if he had expected him to intercede; but his look was riveted on his desk.

"Have you anything to say?" demanded Squeers again, giving his right arm two or three flourishes to try its power and suppleness. "Stand a little out of the way, Mrs. Squeers, my dear; I've hardly got room enough."

"Spare me, sir!" cried Smike.

"Oh! that's all, is it?" said Squeers. "Yes, I'll flog you within an inch of your life, and spare you that."

"Ha! ha! ha!" laughed Mrs. Squeers; "that's a good 'un."

"I was driven to do it," said Smike faintly, and casting another imploring look about him.

E

" Driven to do it, were you ? " said Squeers.   " Oh ! it wasn't your fault ; it was mine, I suppose—eh ? "

" A nasty, ungrateful, pig-headed, brutish, obstinate, sneaking dog ! " exclaimed Mrs. Squeers, taking Smike's head under her arm, and administering a cuff at every epithet.   " What does he mean by that ? "

" Stand aside, my dear," replied Squeers.   " We'll try and find out."

Mrs. Squeers, being out of breath with her exertions, complied.   Squeers caught the boy firmly in his grip ; one desperate cut had fallen on his body—he was wincing from the lash and uttering a scream of pain—it was raised again, and again about to fall —when Nicholas Nickleby, suddenly starting up, cried " Stop ! " in a voice that made the rafters ring.

" Who cried stop ? " said Squeers, turning savagely round.

" I," said Nicholas, stepping forward. " This must not go on."

" Must not go on ! " cried Squeers, almost in a shriek.

" No ! " thundered Nicholas.

Aghast and stupefied by the boldness of the interference,
Squeers released his hold of Smike, and, falling back a pace or
two, gazed upon Nicholas with looks that were positively
frightful.

" I say must not," repeated Nicholas, nothing daunted ;
" shall not.   I will prevent it."

Squeers continued to gaze upon him ; but astonishment had
actually, for the moment, bereft him of speech.

" You have disregarded all my quiet interference in the
miserable lad's behalf," said Nicholas ; " you have returned no
answer to the letter in which I begged forgiveness for him, and
offered to be responsible that he would remain quietly here.
Don't blame me for this public interference.   You have brought
it upon yourself, not I."

" Sit down, beggar ! " screamed Squeers, almost beside
himself with rage, and seizing Smike as he spoke.

" Wretch," rejoined Nicholas fiercely.   " Touch him at your
peril !   I will not stand by and see it done.   My blood is up,
and I have the strength of ten such men as you.   Look to
yourself, for I will not spare you if you drive me on ! "

" Stand back ! " cried Squeers, brandishing his weapon.

" I have a long series of insults to avenge," said Nicholas,
flushed with passion ; " and my indignation is aggravated by the
dastardly cruelties practised on helpless infancy in this foul den.
Have a care, for the consequences shall fall heavily upon your
own head ! "

He had scarcely spoken when Squeers, in a violent outbreak
of wrath, and with a cry like the howl of a wild beast, spat upon
him and struck him a blow across the face with his instrument of
torture, which raised up a bar of livid flesh as it was inflicted.
Smarting with the agony of the blow, and concentrating into that
one moment all his feelings of rage, scorn and indignation,
Nicholas sprang upon him, wrested the weapon from his hand, and,
pinning him by the throat, beat the ruffian till he roared for mercy.

After beating the schoolmaster, Nicholas packed up a few of his things and started off to find his way back to London ; and he had not journeyed far before he was overtaken by Smike, who again had managed to escape. So these two travelled together, with very little money, and meeting with many hardships ; but, for all that, they were happier than they had been in that horrid school.

Nicholas always took the greatest care of Smike, and when after a number of adventures he at last got an appointment as clerk in a merchant's office, he took the poor, friendless lad to live with him and his mother and sister. These were indeed days of happiness, for they were a happy family, though by no means a rich one.

Unfortunately that wicked Squeers would not leave them alone. He was resolved to get Smike back again, for Smike was very useful to him in many ways at Dotheboys Hall. So the schoolmaster laid in wait, and one day caught the unfortunate Smike in the streets of London, and carried him off to his lodgings, meaning to take him back to Yorkshire the next day.

But it so happened there was a Yorkshire farmer at Mr. Squeers' lodgings who knew Smike ; and he took pity on him, and when all was quiet he went to the room where the lad was locked up, and unlocked the door and told him to run away home as fast as he could. And you may be quite sure that Smike took his advice. He was soon at home again with the friends he loved so well.

I am sorry to tell you, however, that this happiness did not last long. Poor Smike began to droop, and became more ill day by day and week by week. And he was always haunted with a fearful dread that that awful man Squeers would pounce upon him again and carry him away. The truth was the poor boy was dying.

And now Nicholas began to see that hope was gone, and that upon the partner of his poverty and the sharer of his better

MR. SQUEERS AND A NEW PUPIL

fortune the world was closing fast. There was little pain, little uneasiness, but there was no rallying, no effort, no struggle for life. He was worn and wasted to the last degree ; his voice had sunk so low that he could scarce be heard to speak. Nature was thoroughly exhausted, and he had lain him down to die.

On a fine, mild autumn day, when all was tranquil and at peace, when the soft sweet air crept in at the open window of the quiet room, and not a sound was heard but the gentle rustling of the leaves, Nicholas sat in his old place by the bedside, and knew that the time was nearly come. So very still it was, that, every now and then, he bent down his ear to listen for the breathing of him who lay asleep, as if to assure himself that life was still there, and that he had not fallen into that deep slumber from which on earth there is no waking.

While he was thus employed, the closed eyes opened, and on the pale face there came a placid smile.

" That's well," said Nicholas. " The sleep has done you good."

" I have had such pleasant dreams," was the answer. " Such pleasant, happy dreams ! "

" Of what ? " said Nicholas.

The dying boy turned towards him, and putting his arm about his neck made answer, " I shall soon be there ! " After a short silence he spoke again. " I am not afraid to die," he said ; " I am quite contented. I almost think that if I could rise from this bed quite well I would not wish to do so now. You have so often told me we shall meet again—so very often lately, and now I feel the truth of that so strongly—that I can even bear to part from you."

The trembling voice and tearful eye, and the closer grasp of the arm which accompanied these latter words, showed how they filled the speaker's heart ; nor were there wanting indications of how deeply they had touched the heart of him to whom they were addressed.

" You say well," returned Nicholas at length, " and comfort

me very much, dear fellow.   Let me hear you say you are happy, if you can."

*   *   *   *   *

They embraced and kissed each other on the cheek.

" Now," he murmured, " I am happy."

He fell into a light slumber, and waking, smiled as before ; then spoke of beautiful gardens, which he said stretched out before him, and were filled with figures of men, women, and many children, all with light upon their faces ; then whispered that it was Eden—and so died.

*   *   *   *   *

One of the strangest things in the poor boy's life was that Nicholas found out some time after that Smike and he were cousins.   Isn't it strange how they had been brought together ?

Now, before finishing this story, perhaps you would like to know what became of Dotheboys Hall and the unfortunate scholars.   Well, Squeers did something more wicked than ever, and was sent to prison, and when the boys heard this they shouted with joy.

Now you must know that the horrible Mrs. Squeers was in the habit of giving all the boys brimstone and treacle, whether they needed it or not.

It was one of the brimstone-and-treacle mornings, and Mrs. Squeers had entered school according to custom with the large bowl and spoon, followed by Miss Squeers and the young Wackford (this was Mr. Squeers' little boy, and a very nasty little boy too), who during his father's absence had taken upon him such minor branches of the executive as kicking the pupils with his nailed boots, pulling the hair of some of the smaller boys, pinching the others in aggravating places, and rendering himself in various similar ways a great comfort and happiness to his mother.   Their entrance, whether by premeditation or a simultaneous impulse, was the signal of revolt.   While one detachment rushed to the door and locked it, and another mounted upon the desks and forms, the newest (and consequently the stoutest) boy seized the cane, and confronting Mrs. Squeers with a stern countenance, snatched off her cap and beaver bonnet, put it on his own head, armed himself with the wooden spoon, and bade her, on pain of death, go down upon her knees and take a dose directly. Before that estimable lady could recover herself or offer the slightest retaliation she was forced into a kneeling posture by a crowd of shouting tormentors, and compelled to swallow a spoonful of the odious mixture, rendered more than usually savoury by the immersion in the bowl of Master Wackford's head, whose ducking was entrusted to another rebel. The success of this first achievement prompted the malicious crowd, whose faces were clustered together in every variety of lank and half-starved ugliness, to further acts of outrage. The leader was insisting

upon Mrs. Squeers repeating her dose, Master Squeers was undergoing another dip in the treacle, and a violent assault had been commenced on Miss Squeers, when suddenly the door was burst open, and in stepped that same Yorkshire farmer that had helped

Smike to run away from Mr. Squeers' lodging in London. The farmer spoke with a peculiar dialect, and I am afraid you would not quite understand it, but this is what he would have said if he had not had a Yorkshire accent :—

"You are nice chaps," said he, looking steadily round. "What's to do here, you young dogs ? "

"Squeers is in prison, and we are going to run away!" cried a score of shrill voices. "We won't stop! we won't stop ! "

"Well then, don't stop," replied the farmer. "Who wants you to stop ? Run away like men, but don't hurt the women."

"Hurrah !" cried the shrill voices more shrilly still.

"Hurrah !" repeated the farmer. "We'll hurrah like men too."

"Hurrah !" cried the voices.

"Another," said the farmer. "Don't be afraid of it. Let's have a good one."

"Hurrah !"

"Now then, let's have one more to end with, and then cut off as quick as you like. Take a good breath now—Squeers is in jail—the school's broken up—it's all over—past and gone—think of that, and let it be a hearty one."

Such a cheer arose as the walls of Dotheboys Hall had never echoed before, and were destined never to respond to again. When the sound had died away the school was empty, and of the busy, noisy crowd which had peopled it but five minutes before, not one remained.

THE RUNAWAY COUPLE

"SUPPOSING a young gentleman not eight years old was to run away with a fine young woman of seven, would you consider that a queer start? That there is a start as I—the Boots at the Holly-Tree Inn—have seen with my own eyes; and I cleaned the shoes they ran away in, and they was so little that I couldn't get my hand into 'em.

"Master Harry Walmers's father, he lived at the Elms, away by Shooter's Hill, six or seven miles from London. He was uncommonly proud of Master Harry, as was his only child; but he didn't spoil him neither. He was a gentleman that had a will of his own, and an eye of his own, and that would be minded. Consequently, though he made quite a companion of the fine bright boy, still he kept the command over him, and the child *was* a child. I was under-gardener there at that time; and one morning Master Harry, he comes to me and says—

F

" 'Cobbs, how should you spell Norah, if you were asked?' and he took out his little knife and began cutting that name in print all over the fence. The next day, as it might be, he stops, along with Miss Norah, where I was hoeing weeds in the gravel, and says, speaking up—

" 'Cobbs, I like you! Why do I like you, do you think, Cobbs? Because Norah likes you.'

" 'Indeed, sir,' says I. 'That's very gratifying.'

" 'Gratifying, Cobbs?' says Master Harry. 'It's better than a million of the brightest diamonds, to be liked by Norah. You're going away, ain't you, Cobbs? Then you shall be our head gardener when we're married.' And he tucks her, in her little sky-blue mantle, under his arm, and walks away.

" I was the Boots at this identical Holly-Tree Inn when one summer afternoon the coach drives up, and out of the coach gets these two children. The young gentleman gets out; hands his lady out; gives the guard something for himself; says to my governor, the landlord: 'We're to stop here to-night, please. Sitting-room and two bedrooms will be required. Mutton chops and cherry pudding for two!' and tucks her under his arm, and walks into the house, much bolder than brass.

" I had seen 'em without their seeing me, and I give the governor my views of the expedition they was upon. 'Cobbs,' says the governor, 'if this is so, I must set off myself and quiet their friends' minds. In which case you must keep your eye upon em, and humour 'em, until I come back. But before I take these measures, Cobbs, I should wish you to find out from themselves whether your opinion is correct.'

"So I goes upstairs, and there I finds Master Harry on an e-normous sofa a-drying the eyes of Miss Norah with his pocket handkercher. Their little legs was entirely off the ground, of course, and it really is not possible to express how small them children looked. 'It's Cobbs! it's Cobbs!' cries Master Harry, and he comes a-running to me, and catching hold of my hand. Miss Norah, she comes running to me on t'other side, and catching hold of my t other hand, and they both jump for joy. And what I had took to be the case was the case.

" 'We're going to be married, Cobbs, at Gretna Green,' says the boy. 'We've run away on purpose. Norah has been in rather low spirits, Cobbs ; but she'll be happy now we have found you to be our friend.'

" I give you my word and honour upon it that, by way of luggage the lady had got a parasol, a smelling bottle, a round and a half of cold buttered toast, eight peppermint drops, and a doll's hairbrush. The gentleman had got about a dozen yards of string, a knife, three or four sheets of writing-paper folded up surprisingly small, a orange, and a chaney mug with his name on it.

" 'What may be the exact nature of your plans, sir ?' says I.

" ' To go on,' replies the boy, ' in the morning, and be married to-morrow.'

" ' Just so, sir. Well, sir, if you will excuse my having the freedom to give an opinion, what I should recommend would be this. I'm acquainted with a pony, sir, which would take you and Mrs. Harry Walmers junior to the end of your journey in a very short space of time. I am not altogether sure, sir, that the pony will be at liberty to-morrow, but even if you had to wait for him it might be worth your while.'

" They clapped their hands and jumped for joy, and called me, ' Good Cobbs ! ' and ' Dear Cobbs ! ' and says I, ' Is there anything you want at present, sir ?'

" ' We should like some cakes after dinner,' answers Mr.
Harry, ' and two apples—and jam. With dinner we should like
to have toast and water. But Norah has always been accustomed
to half a glass of currant wine at dessert, and so have I.'

" ' They shall be ordered, sir,' I answered, and away I went ;
and the way in which all the women in the house went on about
that boy and his bold spirit was a thing to see. They climbed up
all sorts of places to get a look at him, and they peeped, seven
deep, through the keyhole.

" In the evening, after the governor had set off for the Elms,
I went into the room to see how the runaway couple was getting
on. The gentleman was on the window-seat, supporting the lady
in his arms. She had tears upon her face, and was lying very
tired and half asleep, with her head upon his shoulder.

" ' Mrs. Harry Walmers junior fatigued, sir ? '

" ' Yes, she's tired, Cobbs ; she's been in low spirits again ;
she isn't used to being in a strange place, you see. Could you
bring a Norfolk biffin, Cobbs ? I think that would do her good.'

" Well, I fetched the biffin, and Master Harry fed her with a
spoon ; but the lady being heavy with sleep and rather cross, I
suggested bed, and called a chambermaid, but Master Harry must
needs escort her himself, and carry the candle for her. After
embracing her at her own door he retired to his room, where I
softly locked him in.

" They consulted me at breakfast (they had ordered sweet
milk and water, and toast and currant jelly, over night) about the
pony, and I told 'em that it did unfortunately happen that the pony
was half clipped, but that he'd be finished clipping in the course
of the day, and that to-morrow morning at eight o'clock he would
be ready. My own opinion is that Mrs. Harry Walmers junior
was beginning to give in. She hadn't had her hair curled when
she went to bed, and she didn't seem quite up to brushing it
herself, and its getting into her eyes put her out. But nothing
put out Mr. Harry. He sat behind his breakfast cup a-tearing
away at the jelly, as if he'd been his own father.

" In the course of the morning, Master Harry rung the bell
—it was surprising how that there boy did carry on—and said in
a sprightly way, ' Cobbs, is there any good walks in the
neighbourhood ? '

" ' Yes, sir, there's Love Lane.'

" ' Get out with you, Cobbs ! '—that was that there mite's
expression—' you're joking.'

" ' Begging your pardon, sir, there really is a Love Lane,
and a pleasant walk it is ; and proud shall I be to show it to
yourself and Mrs. Harry Walmers junior.'

" Well, I took him down Love Lane to the water meadows,
and there
Master Harry
would have
drowned him-
self in another
minute a-get-
ting out a
water lily for
her. But they
was tired out.
All being so
new and
strange to
them, they
were as tired
as tired could
be. And they
laid down on
a bank of
daisies and
fell asleep.

" They
woke up at
last, and then

one thing was getting pretty clear to me, namely, that Mrs. Harry Walmers junior's temper was on the move. When Master Harry took her round the waist, she said he 'teased her so'; and when he says, 'Norah, my young May moon, your Harry tease you?' she tells him, 'Yes, and I want to go home.'

"A boiled fowl, and baked bread and butter pudding brought Mrs. Walmers up a little; but I could have wished, I must privately own, to have seen her more sensible to the voice of love and less abandoning herself to the currants in the pudding. However, Master Harry, he kep' up, and his noble heart was as fond as ever. Mrs. Walmers turned very sleepy about dusk, and began to cry. Therefore, Mrs. Walmers went off to bed as per yesterday; and Master Harry ditto repeated.

"About eleven at night comes back the governor in a chaise, along of Master Harry's father and a elderly lady. And Master Harry's door being unlocked by me, Master Harry's father goes in, goes up to the bedside, bends gently down, and kisses the little sleeping face. Then he stands looking at it for a moment, looking wonderfully like it; and then he gently shakes the little shoulder. 'Harry, my dear boy! Harry!'

"Master Harry starts up and looks at his pa. Such is the honour of that mite, that he looks at me, too, to see whether he had brought me into trouble.

"'I am not angry, my child. I only want you to dress yourself and come home.'

" ' Yes, pa.' Master Harry dresses himself quick.

" ' Please may I—please, dear pa—may I—kiss Norah before I go ? '

" Master Harry's father he takes Master Harry in his hand, and I leads the way with the candle to that other bedroom where the elderly lady is seated by the bed, and poor little Mrs. Harry Walmers junior is fast asleep. There the father lifts the boy up to the pillow, and he lays his little face down for an instant by the little warm face of poor little Mrs. Harry Walmers junior, and gently draws it to him.

" And that's all about it. Master Harry's father drove away in the chaise having hold of Master Harry's hand. The elderly lady and Mrs. Harry Walmers junior that was never to be (she married a captain long after and went to India) went off next day."

LITTLE PAUL DOMBEY

LITTLE DOMBEY was the son of a rich city merchant. Ever since his marriage, ten years before our story commences, Mr. Dombey had ardently desired to have a son. He was a cold, stern, and pompous man, whose life and interests were entirely absorbed in his business, which appeared to him to be the most important thing in the whole world. It was not so much that he wanted a son to love, and to love him, but because he was so desirous of having one to associate with himself in the business, and make the house once more Dombey and Son in fact, as it was in name, that the little boy who was born to him was so precious, and so eagerly welcome.

There was a pretty little girl of six years old, but her father had taken so little notice of her that it was doubtful if he would have known her had he met her in the street. Of what use was a girl to Dombey and Son? She could not go into the business.

Little Dombey's mother died when he was born, but the event did not greatly disturb Mr. Dombey; and since his son lived, what did it matter to him that his little daughter Florence was breaking her heart in loneliness for the mother who had loved and cherished her!

During the first few months of his life, little Dombey grew and flourished; and as soon as he was old enough to take notice, there was no one he loved so well as his sister Florence. He would laugh and hold out his arms as soon as she came in sight, and the affection of her baby brother comforted the lonely little girl, who was never weary of waiting on and playing with him.

In due time the baby was taken to church, and was given the name of Paul (his father's name). A grand and stately christening it was, followed by a grand and stately feast; and little Paul, when he was brought in to be admired by the company, was declared by his godmother to be " an angel, and the perfect picture of his own papa."

Whether baby Paul caught cold on his christening day or not, no one could tell, but from that time he seemed to waste and pine; his healthy and thriving babyhood had received a check, and as for illnesses, " There never was a blessed dear so put upon," his nurse said. Every tooth had cost him a fit, and as for chicken-pox, whooping-cough, and measles, they followed one upon the other, and to quote Nurse Richards again, " seized and worried him like tiger cats," so that by the time he was five years old, though he had the prettiest, sweetest little face in the world, there was always a patient, wistful look upon it, and he was thin and tiny

G

and delicate.　He would be as merry and full of spirits as other children when playing with Florence in their nursery, but he soon got tired, and had such old-fashioned ways of speaking and doing things, that Richards often shook her head sadly over him.

When he sat in his little arm-chair, with his father after dinner, as Mr. Dombey would have him do every day, they were a strange pair—so like, and so unlike each other.

"What is money, papa?" asked Paul on one of these occasions, crossing his tiny arms as well as he could—just as his father's were crossed.

"Why, gold, silver, and copper; you know what it is well enough, Paul," answered his father.

"Oh yes; I mean what can money do?"

"Anything, everything—almost," replied Mr. Dombey, taking one of his son's wee hands, and beating it softly against his own.

Paul drew his hand gently away.　"It didn't save me my mamma, and it can't make me strong and big," said he.

"Why, you *are* strong and big, as big as such little people usually are," returned Mr. Dombey.

"No," replied Paul sighing; "when Florence was as little as me, she was strong and tall, and did not get tired of playing as I do.　I am *so* tired sometimes, papa."

Mr. Dombey's anxiety was aroused, and he summoned his sister, Mrs. Chick, to consult with him over Paul, and the doctor was sent for to examine him.

"The child is hardly so stout as we could wish," said the doctor; "his mind is too big for his body, he thinks too much—let him try sea air—sea air does wonders for children."

So it was arranged that Florence, Paul, and Nurse should go to Brighton, and stay in the house of a lady named Mrs. Pipchin, who kept a very select boarding-house for children, and whose management of them was said, in the best circles, to be truly marvellous.　Mr. Dombey himself went down to Brighton every week, and had the children to stay with him at his hotel from

Saturday to Monday, that he might judge of the progress made by his son and heir towards health.

There is no doubt that, apart from his importance to the house of Dombey and Son, little Paul had crept into his father's heart, cold though it still was towards his daughter, colder than ever now, for there was in it a sort of unacknowledged jealousy of the warm love lavished on her by Paul, which he himself was unable to win.

Mrs. Pipchin was a marvellously ugly old lady, with a hook nose and stern, cold eyes. Two other children lived at present under her charge, a mild, blue-eyed little girl who was known as Miss Pankey, and a Master Bitherstone, a solemn and sad looking little boy whose parents were in India, and who asked Florence in a depressed voice whether she could give him any idea of the way back to Bengal.

"Well, Master Paul, how do you

think you will like me ? " said Mrs. Pipchin, seeing the child intently regarding her.

" I don't think I shall like you at all," replied Paul, shaking his head. " I want to go away. I do not like your house."

Paul did not like Mrs. Pipchin, but he would sit in his arm-chair and look at her, just as he had looked at his father at home. Her ugliness seemed to fascinate him.

As the weeks went by little Paul grew more healthy-looking, but he did not seem any stronger, and could not run about out of doors. A little carriage was therefore got for him, in which he could be wheeled down to the beach, where he would pass the greater part of the day. He took a great fancy to a queer crab-faced old man, smelling of sea-weed, who wheeled his carriage, and held long conversations with him ; but Florence was the only child-companion whom he ever cared to have with him, though he liked to watch other children playing in the distance. To have Florence sitting by his side, reading or talking to him, whilst the fresh salt wind blew about him, and the little waves rippled up under the wheels of his carriage seemed to perfectly content little Paul.

" I love you, Floy," he said one day to her ; " if you went to India as that boy's sister did, I should die."

Florence laid her head against his pillow, and whispered how much stronger he was growing.

" Oh yes, I know, I am a great deal better," said Paul, " a very great deal better. Listen, Floy ; what is it the sea keeps saying ? "

" Nothing, dear, it is only the rolling of the waves you hear."

" Yes, but they are always saying something, and always the same thing.   What place is over there, Floy ? "

She told him there was another country opposite, but Paul said he did not mean that, he meant somewhere much farther away, oh, much farther away—and often he would break off in the midst of their talk to listen to the sea and gaze out towards that country " farther away."

After having lived at Brighton for a year, Paul was certainly much stronger, though still thin and delicate.   And on one of his weekly visits, Mr. Dombey observed to Mrs. Pipchin, with pompous condescension, " My son is getting on, Madam, he is really getting on.   He is six years of age, and six will be sixteen before we have time to look about us."   And then he went on to explain that Paul's weak health having kept him back in his studies, which, considering the great destiny before the heir of Dombey and Son, was much to be regretted, he had made arrangements to place him at the educational establishment of Dr. Blimber, which was close by.   Florence was, for the present, to remain under Mrs. Pipchin's care, and see her brother every week.

Dr. Blimber's school was a great hothouse for the forcing of boys' brains ;   no matter how backward a boy was, Doctor Blimber could always bring him on, and make a man of him in no time ; and Dr. Blimber promised speedily to make a man of Paul.

" Shall you like to be made a man of, my son ? " asked Mr. Dombey.

" I'd rather be a child and stay with Floy," answered Paul.

Then a different life began for little Dombey.

Miss Blimber, the doctor's daughter, a learned lady in spectacles, was his special tutor, and from morning till night his poor little brains were forced and crammed, till his head was heavy and always had a dull ache in it, and his small legs grew weak again—every day he looked a little thinner and a little paler, and became more old-fashioned than ever in his looks and ways— " old-fashioned " was a distinguishing title which clung to him.

He was gentle and polite to every one—always looking out for small kindnesses which he might do to any inmate of the house. Every one liked " little Dombey," but every one down to the footman said with the same kind of tender smile—he was such an old-fashioned boy. "The oddest and most old-fashioned child in the world," Dr. Blimber would say to his daughter ; "but bring him on, Cornelia—bring him on."

And Cornelia did bring him on ; and Florence, seeing how pale and weary the little fellow looked when he came to her on Saturdays, and how he could not rest from anxiety about his lessons, would lighten his labours a little, and ease his mind by helping him to prepare his week's work. But one day, when his lessons were over, about a fortnight before the commencement of holidays, little Paul laid his weary and aching head against the knee of a school-fellow of whom he was very fond, and somehow forgot to lift it up again ; and the first thing he noticed when he opened his eyes was that the window was open, his face and hair were wet with water, and that Dr. Blimber and the usher were both standing looking at him.

"Ah, that's well," said Dr. Blimber as Paul opened his eyes, "and how is my little friend now ? "

" Oh, quite well, thank you, sir," answered Paul, but when he got up there seemed something the matter with the floor, and the walls were dancing about, and Dr. Blimber's head was twice its natural size. Toots, the schoolfellow against whom Paul had been leaning, took him up in his arms, and very kindly helped him to bed, and presently the doctor came and looked at him, and said he was not to do any more lessons for the present.

In a few days Paul was able to get up and creep about the house. He wondered sometimes why every one looked at and spoke so very kindly to him, and was more than ever careful to do any little kindnesses he could think of for them : even the rough, ugly dog, Diogenes, who lived in the yard, came in for a share of his attentions.

There was to be a party at Dr. Blimber's on the evening before the boys went home, and Paul wished to remain for this, because Florence was coming, and he wanted her to see how every one was fond of him. He was to go away with her after the party. Paul sat in a corner of the sofa all the evening, and every one was very kind to him indeed, it was quite extraordinary, Paul thought, and he was very happy ; he liked to see how pretty Florence was, and how every one admired and wished to dance with her. When the time came for them to take leave, the whole houseful gathered on the steps to say good-bye to little Dombey and his sister, Toots even opening the carriage door to say it over again. After resting for a night at Mrs. Pipchin's house, little Paul went home, and was carried straight upstairs to his bed. " Floy, dear," said he to his sister, when he was comfortably settled, " was that papa in the hall when I was carried in ? "

" Yes, dear," answered Florence.

" He didn't cry, did he, Floy, and go into his own room when he saw me ? " Florence could only shake her head, and hide her face against his, as she kissed him.

" I should not like to think papa cried," murmured little Paul as he went to sleep. He lay in his bed day after day quite happily and patiently, content to watch and talk to Florence. He would tell her his dreams, and how he always saw the sunlit ripples of a river rolling, rolling fast in front of him ; sometimes he seemed to be rocking in a little boat on the water, and its motion lulled him to rest, and then he would be floating away, away to that shore farther off, which he could not see. One day he told Florence that the water was rippling brighter and faster than ever, and that he could not see anything else.

" My own boy, cannot you see your poor father ? " said Mr. Dombey, bending over him.

" Oh yes ; but don't be so sorry, dear papa, I am so happy,— good-bye, dear papa." Presently he opened his eyes again, and said, " Floy, mamma is like you ; I can see her. Come close to me, Floy, and tell them," whispered the dying boy, " that the face of the picture of Christ on the staircase at school is not divine enough ; the light from it is shining on me now, and the water is shining too, and rippling so fast, so fast." The evening light shone into the room, but little Paul's spirit had gone out on the rippling water, and the Divine Face was shining on him from the farther shore.

LITTLE NELL AND HER GRANDFATHER

THE house was one of those receptacles for old and curious things, which seem to crouch in odd corners of London town ; and in the old, dark, murky rooms, there lived together, alone, an old man and a child—his grandchild, little Nell. Solitary and monotonous as was her life, the innocent and cheerful spirit of the child found happiness in all things, and through the dim rooms of the old curiosity shop little Nell went singing, moving with gay and lightsome step.

But gradually over the old man, to whom she was so tenderly attached, there stole a sad change. He became thoughtful,

H

dejected, and wretched.   He had no sleep nor rest but that which he took by day in his easy chair ; for every night, and all night long, he was away from home.   To the child it seemed that her grandfather's love for her increased, even with the hidden grief by which she saw him struck down.   And to see him sorrowful, and not to know the cause of his sorrow ; to see him growing pale and weak, under his agony of mind, so weighed upon her gentle spirit, that at times she felt as though her heart must break.

At last the time came when the old man's feeble frame could bear up no longer against his hidden care.   A raging fever seized him, and as he lay delirious or insensible through many weeks, Nell learned that the house which sheltered them was theirs no longer ; that in the future they would be very poor ; that they would scarcely have bread to eat.

At length the old man began to mend, but his mind was weakened.

He would sit for hours together, with Nell's small hand in his, playing with the fingers, and sometimes stopping to smooth her hair or kiss her brow ; and when he saw that tears were glistening in her eyes he would look amazed.   As the time drew near when they must leave the house, he made no reference to the necessity of finding other shelter.   An indistinct idea he had, that the child was desolate, and in need of help ; though he seemed unable to contemplate their real position more distinctly.   But a change came upon him one evening, as he and Nell sat quietly together.

" Let us speak softly, Nell," he said.   " Hush ! for if they knew our purpose they would say that I was mad, and take thee from me.   We will not stop here another day.   We will travel afoot through the fields and woods, and trust ourselves to God in places where He dwells.   To-morrow morning, dear, we'll turn our faces from this scene of sorrow, and be as free and happy as the birds."

The child's heart beat high with hope and confidence.   She had no thought of hunger, or cold, or thirst, or suffering.   To her

LITTLE NELL

it seemed that they might beg their way from door to door in happiness, so that they were together.

When the day began to glimmer they stole out of the house, and passing into the street stood still.

"Which way?" asked the child.

The old man looked irresolutely and helplessly at her, and shook his head. It was plain that she was thenceforth his guide and leader. The child felt it, but had no doubts nor misgivings, and, putting her hand in his, led him away. Forth from the city, while it yet slumbered, went the two poor adventurers, wandering they knew not whither.

They passed through the long, deserted streets, in the glad light of early morning, until these streets dwindled away, and the open country was about them. They walked all day, and slept that night at a small cottage where beds were let to travellers. The sun was setting on the second day of their journey, and they were jaded and worn out with walking, when, following a path which led through a churchyard to the town where they were to spend the night, they fell in with two travelling showmen, exhibitors of a Punch and Judy show, bound for the races at a neighbouring town. And with these men they travelled forward on the following day.

They made two long days' journey with their new companions, passing through villages and towns, and meeting upon one occasion with two young people walking upon stilts, who were also going to the races. The men were rough and strange, as it seemed to little Nell, in their ways, but they were kindly, too; and in the tumult and confusion of such scenes as she had never known before, and in the bewildering noise and movement of the race-course, where she tried to sell some little nosegays, Nell would have clung to them for protection, had she not learned that these men suspected that she and the old man had left their home secretly, and that they meant to take steps to have them sent back and taken care of. Separation from her grandfather was the greatest evil Nell could dread. If they should be found (so

the child thought), people would shut him from the light of sun and sky, saying that he was mad, and never let her see him more. She seized her opportunity to evade the watchfulness of the two men, and hand in hand she and the old man fled away together.

That night they reached a little village in a woody hollow. The village schoolmaster, a good and gentle man, pitying their weariness, and attracted by the child's sweetness and modesty, gave them a lodging for the night ; nor would he let them leave until two days more had passed.

They journeyed on, when the time came that they must wander forth again, by pleasant country lanes ; and as they passed, watching the birds that perched and twittered in the branches overhead, or listening to the songs that broke the happy silence, their hearts were tranquil and serene. But by-and-bye they came to a long, winding road which lengthened out far into the distance, and though they still kept on, it was at a much slower pace, for they were now very weary and fatigued. The afternoon had worn away into a beautiful evening, when they came to a caravan drawn up by the road. It was a smart little house upon wheels, and at the door sat a stout and comfortable lady, taking tea. The tea-things were set out upon a drum, covered with a white napkin. And there, as if at the most convenient table in the world, sat this roving lady, taking her tea and enjoying the prospect. Of this stout lady Nell ventured to ask how far it was to the neighbouring town. And the lady, being kind-hearted, and noticing that the tired child could hardly repress a tear at hearing that eight weary miles lay still before them, not only gave them tea, but offered to take them on in the caravan.

Now this lady of the caravan was the owner of a waxwork show, and her name was Mrs. Jarley. And Mrs. Jarley was won, as the poor schoolmaster had been, by Nell's gentle looks and manner. She offered Nell employment in pointing out the figures in the waxwork show to the visitors who came to see it, promising in return both board and lodging for the child and her grandfather, and some small sum of money. This offer Nell was thankful to accept, and for some time her life and that of the poor, vacant, fond old man, passed quietly and almost happily.

But heavier sorrow was yet to come. One night, a holiday night for them, Nell and her grandfather went out to walk. A terrible thunderstorm coming on, they were forced to take refuge in a small public-house; and here some sinister and ill-favoured men were playing cards. The old man watched them with increasing interest and excitement, until his whole appearance underwent a complete change. His face was flushed and eager, his teeth set. With a hand that trembled violently, he seized Nell's little purse, and in spite of her entreaties joined in the game, gambling with such a savage thirst for gain that the distressed and frightened child could almost better have borne to see him dead. The night was far advanced before the play came to an end, and they were forced to remain where they were until the morning. And in the night the child was wakened from her troubled sleep to find a figure in the room—a figure busying its hands about her garments, while its face was turned to her, listening and looking lest she should awake. It was her grandfather himself, his white face pinched and sharpened by the greediness which made his eyes unnaturally bright, counting the money of which his hands were robbing her.

Evening after evening, after that night, the old man would creep away, not to return until the night was far spent, demanding, wildly, money. And at last there came an hour when the child overheard him, tempted beyond his feeble powers of resistance, undertake to find more money, to feed the desperate passion which had laid its hold upon his weakness, by robbing Mrs. Jarley.

That night the child took her grandfather by the hand and led him forth. Through the straight streets and narrow outskirts of the town their trembling feet passed quickly; the child sustained by one idea—that they were flying from disgrace and crime, and that her grandfather's preservation must depend solely upon her firmness unaided by one word of advice or any helping hand; the old man following her as though she had been an angel messenger sent to lead him where she would.

The hardest part of all their wanderings was now before them. They slept in the open air that night, and on the following morning some men offered to take them a long distance on their barge. These men, though they were not unkindly, were very rugged, noisy fellows, and they drank and quarrelled fearfully among themselves, to Nell's inexpressible terror. It rained, too, heavily, and she was wet and cold. At last they reached the great city whither the barge was bound, and here they wandered up and down, being now penniless, and watched the faces of those who passed, to find among them a ray of encouragement or hope. Ill in body, and sick to death at heart, the child needed her utmost firmness and resolution even to creep along.

They lay down that night, and the next night too, with nothing between them and the sky; a penny loaf was all they had had that day, and when the third morning came, it found the child much weaker, yet she made no complaint. The great manufacturing city hemmed them in on every side, and seemed to shut out hope. Faint and spiritless as they were, its streets were insupportable; and the child, throughout the remainder of that hard day, compelled herself to press on, that they might reach the country. Evening was drawing on; they were dragging themselves through the last street, and she felt that the time was close at hand when her enfeebled powers would bear no more. Seeing a traveller on foot before them, and animated with a ray of hope, she shot on before her grandfather, and began in a few faint words to implore the stranger's help. He turned his head, the child clapped her hands together, uttered a wild shriek, and fell senseless

at his feet. It was the village schoolmaster who had been so
kind to them before.

And now Nell's weary wanderings were nearly over. The
good man took her in his arms and carried her quickly to a little

inn hard by, where she was tenderly put to bed, and where a doctor arrived with all speed. The schoolmaster, as it appeared, was on his way to a new home. And when the child had recovered somewhat from her exhaustion, it was arranged that she and her grandfather should accompany him to the village whither he was bound, and that he should endeavour to find them some humble occupation by which they could subsist.

It was a secluded village, lying among the quiet country scenes Nell loved. And here, her grandfather being tranquil and at rest, a great peace fell upon the spirit of the child. Often she would steal into the church, and sitting down among the quiet figures carved upon the tombs, would think of the summer days and the bright spring time that would come ; of the rays of sun that would fall in, aslant those sleeping forms ; of the songs of birds, and the sweet air that would steal in. What if the spot awakened thoughts of death ? It would be no pain to sleep amid such sights and sounds as these. For the time was drawing nearer every day when Nell was to rest indeed. She never murmured or complained, but faded like a light upon a summer's evening and died. Day after day and all day long, the old man, broken-hearted and with no love or care for anything in life, would sit beside her grave with her straw hat and the little basket she had been used to carry, waiting till she should come to him again. At last they found him lying dead upon the stone. And in the church where they had often prayed and mused and lingered, hand in hand, the child and the old man slept together.

I

POOR JO, THE CROSSING-SWEEPER

JO was a crossing-sweeper; his crossing was in Holborn, and there every day he swept up the mud, and begged for pennies from the people who passed. Poor Jo wasn't at all pleasant to look at. He wasn't pretty and he wasn't clean. His clothes were only a few poor rags that hardly protected him from the cold and the rain. He had never been to school, and he could neither write nor read—could not even spell his own name. He had only one name, Jo, and that served him for Christian and surname too.

Poor Jo! He was ugly and dirty and ignorant; but he knew one thing, that it was wicked to tell a lie, and knowing this, he always told the truth. One other thing poor Jo knew too well, and that was what being hungry means. For little Jo was very poor. He lived in Tom-all-Alones, one of the most horrible places in all London. The road here is thick with mud. The crazy houses are dropping away ; two of them, Jo remembered, once fell to pieces. The air one breathes here is full of fever. The people who live in this dreadful den are the poorest of London poor. All miserably clad, all dirty, all very hungry. They know and like Jo, for he is always willing to go on errands for them, and does them many little acts of kindness. Not that they speak of him as Jo.

Oh, dear no ! No one in Tom-all-Alones is spoken of by his name, whether it be his surname, or that which his godfathers and godmothers—always supposing that he had any—gave him. The ladies and gentlemen who live in this unfashionable neighbourhood have their fashions just as much as the great folks who live in the grand mansions in the West End. Here one of the prevailing customs is to give every one a nickname. Thus it is that if you inquired there for a boy named Jo, you would be asked whether you meant Carrots, or the Colonel, or Gallows, or young Chisel, or Terrier Tip, or Lanky, or the Brick.

Jo was generally called Toughy, although a few superior persons who gave themselves airs and graces, and affected a dignified style of speaking, called him " the tough subject."

Jo used to say he had never had but one friend.

It was one cold winter night, when he was shivering in a doorway near his crossing, that a dark-haired, rough-bearded man turned to look at him, and then came back and began to talk to him.

" Have you a friend, boy ? " he asked presently.

" No, never 'ad none."

" Neither have I. Not one. Take this, and Good-night," and so saying, the man who looked very poor and shabby put into Jo's hand the price of a supper and a night's lodging.

Often afterwards the stranger would stop to talk with Jo, and give him money, Jo firmly believed, whenever he had any to give. When he had none, he would merely say, " I am as poor as you are to-day, Jo," and pass on.

One day Jo was fetched away from his crossing by the beadle, and taken by him to the " Sol's Arms," a public-house in a little court near Chancery Lane, where the Coroner was holding an Inquest—an " Inkwich " Jo called it.

" Did the boy know the deceased ? " asked the Coroner.

Indeed Jo had known him ; it was his only friend who was dead.

" He was wery good to me, he was," said poor Jo.

The next day they buried the dead man in the churchyard hard by ; a churchyard hemmed in by houses on either side, and separated by an iron gate from the wretched court through which one goes to it.

But that night there came a slouching figure through the court to the iron gate. It held the gate with both hands and looked between the bars—stood looking in for a little while, then with an old broom it softly swept the step and made the archway clean. It was poor Jo ; and as, after one more long look through the bars of the gate, he went away, he softly said to himself, " He was wery good to me, he was."

Now, there happened to be at the Inquest a kind-hearted little man named Snagsby, who was a stationer by trade, and he pitied Jo so much that he gave him half-a-crown. Half-a-crown was Mr. Snagsby's one remedy for all the troubles of this world.

Jo was very sad after the death of his only friend. The more so as his friend had died in great poverty and misery, with no one near him to care whether he lived or not.

It was a few days after the funeral, while Jo was still living on Mr. Snagsby's half-crown—half a bill Jo called it—that a much bigger slice of good luck fell to his share. He was standing at his crossing as the day closed in, when a lady, closely veiled and plainly dressed, came up to him.

" Are you the boy Jo who was examined at the Inquest ? " she asked.

" That's me," said Jo.

" Come farther up the court, I want to speak to you."

" Wot, about him as was dead ?   Did you know him ? "

" How dare you ask me if I knew him ? "

" No offence, my lady," said Jo humbly.

" Listen and be silent.   Show me the place where he lived, then where he died, then where they buried him.   Go in front of me, don't look back once, and I'll pay you well."

" I'm fly," said Jo.   " But fen larks, you know.   Stow hooking it ! "

Jo takes her to each of the places she wants to see, and he notices that when he shows her the burying-place she shrinks into a dark corner as if to hide herself while she looks at the spot where the dead man's body rests.   Then she draws off her glove, and Jo sees that she has sparkling rings on her fingers.   She drops a coin into his hand and is gone.   Jo holds the coin to the light and sees to his joy that it is a golden sovereign.   He bites it to make sure that it is genuine, and being satisfied that it has successfully stood the test, he puts it under his tongue for safety, and goes off to Tom-all-Alones.

But people in Jo's position in life find it hard to change a sovereign, for who will believe that they can come by it honestly ? So poor little Jo didn't get much of the sovereign for himself, for, as he afterwards told Mr. Snagsby—

" I had to pay five bob down in Tom-all-Alones before they'd square it for to give me change, and then a young man he thieved another five while I was asleep, and a boy he thieved ninepence, and the landlord he stood drains round with a lot more of it."

And so Jo was left alone in the world again, now his friend was dead.   And this poor friend had only two mourners, Jo the crossing-sweeper, and the lady who had come to look at his grave.

Jo mourned for him because he had been his only friend, and the lady mourned for the poor man because she had loved him dearly many years ago when they had both been young together.

As time went on Jo's troubles began in earnest. The police turned him away from his crossing, and wheresoever they met him ordered him "to move on." It was hard, very hard on poor Jo; for he knew no way of getting a living except at his crossing. So he would go back to it as often as he dared, until the police turned him away again. Once a policeman, angry to find that Jo hadn't moved on, seized him by the arm and dragged him down to Mr. Snagsby's.

"What's the matter, constable?" asked Mr. Snagsby.

"This boy's as obstinate a young gonogh as I know; although repeatedly told to, he won't move on."

"I'm always a-moving on," cried Jo. "Oh, my eye, where am I to move to?"

"My instructions don't go to that," the constable answered; "my instructions are that you're to keep moving on. Now the simple question is, sir," turning to Mr. Snagsby, "whether you know him. He says you do."

"Yes, I know something of him, but no harm."

After again cautioning Jo to keep moving on, though to where he still did not say, the constable then moved on himself, leaving Jo at Mr. Snagsby's. There was a little tea-party there that evening, and one of the guests, a very greasy, oily-looking man, whom they called Mr. Chadband, and who was a dissenting minister, having by this time eaten and drunk a great deal more than was good for him, determined to improve the occasion by delivering a discourse on Jo. It was very long and very dull to Jo: and in it was this couplet—

"O running stream of sparkling joy,
   To be a soaring human boy."

What Jo liked the best was, when the perspiring Chadband had finished, and he was at last allowed to go, Mr. Snagsby followed him to the door and filled his hands with the remains of the little feast they had had upstairs.

And now Jo began to find life harder and rougher than ever. He lost his crossing altogether, and spent day after day in moving on. He grew hungrier and thinner, and at last the foul air of Tom-all-Alones began to have an ill-effect even on him—"the tough subject." His throat grew very dry, his cheeks were burning hot, and his poor little head ached till the pain made him cry. Then he remembered a poor woman he had once done a kindness to, a brickmaker's wife, who had told him she lived at St. Albans, and that a lady there had been very good to her. "Perhaps she'll be good to me," thought Jo, and he started off to go to St. Albans. So it came about that one Saturday night Jo reached that town very tired and very ill. Happily for him the brickmaker's wife met him and took him into her cottage. While he was resting there a lady came in.

The lady sat down by the bed, and asked him very kindly what was the matter.

"I'm a-being froze and then burnt up, and then froze and burnt up again, ever so many times over in an hour. And my head's all sleepy, and all a-going round like, and I'm so dry, and my bones is nothing half so much bones as pain."

"Where are you going?"

"Somewheres," replied Jo, "I'm a-being moved on, I am."

"Well, to-night you must come with me, and I'll make you comfortable." So Jo went with the lady to a great house not far off, and there in a nice warm loft they made a bed for him, and brought him tempting, wholesome food. Everyone was very kind to him, even the servants called him "Old Chap," and told him he would soon be well. Jo was really happy, and for a time forgot his pain and fever. But something frightened Jo, and he felt he could not stay there, and he ran out into the cold night air. Where he went he could never remember, for when he next came to his senses he found himself in a hospital. He stayed there for some weeks, and was then discharged, though still weak and ill. He was very thin, and when he drew a breath his chest was very painful. "It draws," said Jo, "as heavy as a cart."

Now, a certain young doctor who was very kind to poor people, was walking through Tom-all-Alones one morning, when he saw a ragged figure coming along, crouching close to the dirty wall. The figure shrank along with its shapeless clothes hanging to it. It was Jo. The young doctor took pity on Jo. "Come with me," he said, "and I will find you a better place than this to stay in," for he saw that the lad was very, very ill. So Jo was taken to a clean little room, and bathed, and had clean clothes, and good food, and kind people about him once more, but he was too ill now, far too ill, for anything to do him any good.

"Let me lie here quiet," said poor Jo, "and be so kind anyone as is passin' nigh where I used to sweep, as to say to Mr. Snagsby as Jo, wot he knew once, is a-moving on."

One day the young doctor was sitting by him, when suddenly Jo made a strong effort to get out of bed.

"Stay, Jo—where now?"

"It's time for me to go to that there burying-ground."

"What burying-ground, Jo?"

"Where they laid him as was wery good to me, wery good to me, indeed he was. It's time for me to go down to that there burying-ground, sir, and ask to be put along of him. I wants to go there and be buried. He used for to say to me, 'I am as poor to-day as you, Jo,' he says. I want to tell him that I am as poor as him now, and I want

to be along with him." " By-and-by, Jo, by-and-by."

"Ah, perhaps they wouldn't do it, if I was to go by myself. But will you promise to have me took there, and laid along with him ? " " I will indeed." "Thankee, sir. There's a step there as I used to sweep with my broom. It's turned very dark, sir ; is there any light coming ? " " It's coming fast, Jo." Then silence for a while. " Jo, my poor fellow——!" " I can hear you, sir, in the dark." " Jo, can you say what I say ? " " I'll say anythink you say, sir, for I knows it's good." " Our Father." " Our Father— yes, that's very good, sir." " Which art in Heaven." " Art in Heaven. Is the light a-coming, sir ? " " It's close at hand. Hallowed be Thy Name." " Hallowed be Thy——"

The light had come. Oh yes ! the light had come, for Jo was dead.

K

LITTLE   DAVID   COPPERFIELD

LITTLE DAVID COPPERFIELD lived with his mother in
a pretty house in the village of Blunderstone in Suffolk.
He had never known his father, who died before David could
remember anything, and he had neither brothers nor sisters.   He
was fondly loved by his pretty young mother, and their kind,
good servant Peggotty, and David was a very happy little fellow.
They had very few friends, and the only relation Mrs. Copperfield
talked about was an aunt of David's father, a tall and rather
terrible lady, from all accounts, who had once been to see them
when David was quite a tiny baby and had been so angry

to find David was not a little girl, that she had left the house quite offended, and had never been heard of since. One visitor, a tall, dark gentleman, David did not like at all, and he was rather inclined to be jealous that his mother should be friendly with the stranger.

One day Peggotty, the servant, asked David if he would like to go with her on a visit to her brother at Yarmouth.

" Is your brother an agreeable man, Peggotty ? " he enquired.

" Oh, what an agreeable man he is ! " cried Peggotty. " Then there's the sea, and the boats and ships, and the fishermen, and the beach. And 'Am to play with."

Ham was her nephew. David was quite anxious to go when he heard of all these delights ; but his mother ; what would she do all alone ? Peggotty told him his mother was going to pay a visit to some friends, and would be sure to let him go. So all was arranged, and they were to start the next day in the carrier's cart. David was so eager that he wanted to put his hat and coat on the night before ! But when the time came to say good-bye to his dear mamma, he cried a little, for he had never left her before. It was rather a slow way of travelling, and poor David was very tired and sleepy when they arrived at Yarmouth, and found Ham waiting to meet them. He was a great strong fellow, six feet high, and took David on his back and the box under his arm to carry both to the house. David was delighted to find that this house was made of a real big black boat, with a door and windows cut in the side, and an iron funnel sticking out of the roof for a chimney. Inside, it was very cosy and clean, and David had a tiny bedroom in the stern. He was much pleased to find a dear little girl, about his own age, to play with, and soon discovered that she and Ham were orphan cousins, children of Mr. Peggotty's brother and sister, whose fathers had both been drowned at sea, so kind Mr. Peggotty had taken them to live with him. An elderly woman, named Mrs. Gummidge, lived with them too, and did the cooking and cleaning, for she was a poor widow and had no home of her own. David thought Mr.

Peggotty was very good to take all these people to live with him and he was quite right, for Mr. Peggotty was only a poor man himself and had to work hard to get a living.   David was very happy in this queer house, playing on the beach with Em'ly, as they called the little girl, and he told her all about his happy home ; and she told him how her father had been drowned at sea before she came to live with her uncle.

David said he thought Mr. Peggotty must be a very good man.

"Good !" said Em'ly.   "If ever I was to be a lady, I'd give him a sky-blue coat with diamond buttons, nankeen trousers, a red velvet waistcoat, a cocked hat, a large gold watch, a silver pipe, and a box of money !"

David was quite sorry to leave these kind people and his dear little companion, but still he was glad to think he should get back to his own dear mamma.   When he reached home, however, he found a great change.   His mother was married to the dark man David did not like, whose name was Mr. Murdstone, and he was a stern, hard man, who had no love for little David, and did not allow his mother to pet and indulge him as she had done before.   Mr. Murdstone's sister came to live with them, and as she was even more difficult to please than her brother, and disliked boys, David's life was no longer a happy one.   He tried to be good and obedient, for he knew it made his mother very unhappy to see him punished and found fault with.   He had always had lessons with his mother, and as she was patient and gentle, he had enjoyed learning to read, but now he had a great many very hard lessons to do, and was so frightened and shy when Mr. and Miss Murdstone were in the room, that he did not get on at all well, and was continually in disgrace.   His only pleasure was to go up into a little room at the top of the house where he had found a number of books that had belonged to his own father, and he would sit and read Robinson Crusoe, and many tales of travels and adventures, and he imagined himself to be the heroes, and went about for days with the centre-piece out of an old set of

LITTLE EMLY AND MR PEGGOTTY

boot-trees, pretending to be a Captain in the British Royal Navy.

But one day he got into sad trouble over his lessons, and Mr. Murdstone was very angry, and took him away from his mother and beat him with a cane. David had never been beaten in his life before, and was so maddened by the pain and by rage that he bit Mr. Murdstone's hand! Now, indeed, he had done something to deserve the punishment, and Mr. Murdstone, in a fury, beat him savagely, and left him sobbing and crying on the floor, with a dreadful feeling in his heart of how wicked and full of hate he was. David was kept locked up in his room for some days, seeing no one but Miss Murdstone, who brought him his food. At last, one night, he heard his name whispered at the keyhole.

"Is that you, Peggotty?" he asked, groping his way to the door.

"Yes, my precious Davy. Be as soft as a mouse or the cat will hear us."

David understood she meant Miss Murdstone, whose room was quite near. "How's mamma, Peggotty dear? Is she very angry with me?" he whispered. Peggotty was crying softly on her side of the door as David was on his.

"No—not very," she said.

"What is going to be done with me, dear Peggotty, do you know?" asked poor David, who had been wondering all these long, lonely days.

"School—near London—"

"When, Peggotty?"

"To-morrow," answered Peggotty.

"Shan't I see mamma?"

"Yes—morning," she said, and went on to promise David she would always love him, and take the greatest care of his dear mamma, and write to him every week.

"Thank you, thank you, dear Peggotty, and do write and tell Mr. Peggotty, and Em'ly and Ham and Mrs. Gummidge, that I am not so bad as they might suppose, and give them all my love.   Will you, please, Peggotty?"

Peggotty promised, and they both kissed the keyhole most tenderly, and parted.

The next morning David saw his mother, very pale and with red eyes.   He ran to her arms and begged her to forgive him.

" Oh, Davy," she said, "that you should hurt anyone I love ! I forgive you, Davy, but it grieves me so that you should have such bad passions in your heart.   Try to be better, pray to be better."

David was very unhappy that his mother should think him so wicked and though she kissed him and said, " I forgive you, my dear boy, God bless you," he cried so bitterly when he was on his way in the carrier's cart, that his pocket handkerchief had to be spread out on the horse's back to dry.

After they had gone a little way the cart stopped, and Peggotty came running up with a parcel of cakes and a purse for David.   After giving him a good hug, she ran off.

David found three bright shillings in the purse, and two half-crowns wrapped in paper on which was written, in his mother's hand—" For Davy.   With my love."

David shared the cakes with the carrier, who asked if Peggotty made them, and David told him yes, she did all their cooking.   The carrier looked thoughtful, and then asked David if he would send a message to Peggotty from him.   David agreed, and the message was " Barkis is willing."   While David was waiting for the coach at Yarmouth, he wrote to Peggotty.

" My Dear Peggotty,—I have come here safe.   Barkis is willing.   My love to mamma.—Yours affectionately.

" P.S.—He says he particularly wanted you to know *Barkis is willing.*"

At Yarmouth he found dinner was ordered for him, and felt very shy at having a table all to himself, and very much alarmed when the waiter told him he had seen a gentleman fall down dead after drinking some of their beer.   David said he would have some water, and was quite grateful to the waiter for drinking the ale that had been ordered for him, for fear the people of the hotel should be offended. The waiter also helped David to eat his dinner, and accepted one of his bright shillings.

After a long, tiring journey by the coach, for there were no trains in those days, David arrived in London and was taken to a school at Blackheath, by one of the masters, Mr. Mell.

When they got to Salem House, as the school was called, David found the holidays were not over, but that he had been sent before the school was opened as a punishment for his wickedness, and was also to wear a placard on his back, on which was written—" Take care of him. He bites." This made David miserable, and he dreaded the return of the boys. Fortunately for David, the first boy who came back, Tommy Traddles, was not an unkind boy, and seemed to think the placard rather a joke and showed it to all the boys as they came back, with the remark—

"Look here—here's a game!"

Some of the boys teased David by pretending he was a dog, calling him Towser, and patting and stroking him; but, on the whole, it was not so bad as David had expected. The head boy, too, Steerforth, who was very handsome and some years older than David, said he thought it was "a jolly shame" when he heard all about David's punishment, which consoled the little boy very much. Steerforth promised to take care of him, and David loved him dearly, and thought him a great hero. Steerforth took a particular fancy to the pretty, bright-eyed little fellow, and David became a favourite with the boys, by telling them all he could remember of the tales he had read. He spent all his money the first day on a grand supper in their bedroom (by Steerforth's advice), and heard many things about the school, and how severe Mr. Creakle, the head master, was. This he found was very true, and the boys were always being caned and punished, especially poor Traddles, who often suffered from his firmly refusing ever to betray any of his schoolfellows.

One day David had a visit from Mr. Peggotty and Ham, who brought two enormous lobsters, a huge crab, and a large canvas bag of shrimps, as they "remembered he was partial to a relish with his meals."

David was proud to introduce his friend Steerforth to these kind simple friends, and told them how good Steerforth was to him, and how he helped him with his work and took care of him, and Steerforth delighted the fishermen with his friendly, pleasant manners.

The "relish" was much appreciated by the boys at supper that night. Only poor Traddles became very ill from eating crab so late.

At last the holidays came, and David went home. The carrier, Barkis, met him at Yarmouth, and was rather gruff, which David soon found out was because he had not had any answer to his message. David promised to ask Peggotty for one. When he got home David found he had a little baby brother, and his mother and Peggotty were very much pleased to see him again. They had a very happy afternoon the day he came. Mr. and Miss Murdstone were out, and David sat with his mother and Peggotty, and told them all about his school and Steerforth, and took the little baby in his arms and nursed it lovingly. But when the Murdstones came back, David was more unhappy than ever, for they showed plainly they disliked him, and thought him in the way, and scolded him, and would not allow him to touch the baby, or even to sit with Peggotty in the kitchen, so he was not sorry when the time came for him to go back to school, except for leaving his dear mamma and the baby. She kissed him very tenderly at parting, and held up the baby for him to see as he drove off in the carrier's cart once more.

About two months after he had been back at school he was sent for one day to go into the parlour. He hurried in joyfully, for it was his birthday, and he thought it might be a hamper from Peggotty—but, alas! no ; it was very sad news Mrs. Creakle had to give him—his dear mamma had died! Mrs. Creakle was very kind and gentle to the desolate little boy, and the boys, especially Traddles, were very sorry for him.

David went home the next day, and heard that the dear baby had died too. Peggotty received him with great tenderness, and told him about his mother's illness and how she had sent a loving message.

"Tell my dearest boy that his mother, as she lay here, blessed him not once, but a thousand times," and she had prayed to God to protect and keep her fatherless boy.

Mr. Murdstone did not take any notice of poor little David, nor had Miss Murdstone a word of kindness for the orphan. Peggotty was to leave in a month, and, to their great joy, David was allowed to go with her on a visit to Mr. Peggotty. On their way David found out that the mysterious message he had given to Peggotty meant that Barkis wanted to marry her, and Peggotty had consented. Everyone in Mr. Peggotty's cottage was pleased to see David, and did their best to comfort him. Little Em'ly was at school when he arrived, and he went out to meet her, but when he saw her coming along, her blue eyes bluer, and her bright face prettier than ever, he pretended not to know her, and was passing by, when Em'ly laughed and ran away, so of course he was obliged to run and catch her, and try to kiss her, but she would not let him, saying she was not a baby now. But she was kind to him all the same, and when they spoke about the loss of his dear mother, David saw that her eyes were full of tears.

" Ah," said Mr. Peggotty, running his fingers through her bright curls, " here's another orphan, you see, sir, and here," giving Ham a backhanded knock in the chest, " is another of 'em, though he don't look much like it."

" If I had *you* for a guardian, Mr. Peggotty," said David, " I don't think I should *feel* much like it."

" Well said, Master Davy, bor ! " cried Ham delighted. " Hoorah, well said ! no more you wouldn't, bor, bor ! " returning Mr. Peggotty's backhander, while little Em'ly got up and kissed her uncle.

During this visit Peggotty was married to Mr. Barkis, and had a nice little house of her own, and David spent the night before he was to return home in a little room in the roof.

"Young or old, Davy dear, so long as I have this house over my head," said Peggotty, " you shall find it as if I expected you here directly every minute. I shall keep it as I used to keep your old little room, my darling, and if you was to go to China, you might think of its being kept just the same all the time you were away."

David felt how good and true a friend she was, and thanked her as well as he could, for they had brought him to the gate of his home, and Peggotty had him clasped in her arms.

Poor little lonely David, with no one near to speak a loving word, or a face to look on his with love or liking, only the two persons who had broken his mother's heart to live with. How utterly wretched and forlorn he felt! He found he was not to go back to school any more, and wandered about sad and solitary, neglected and uncared for. Peggotty's weekly visits were his only comfort. He longed to go to school, however hard an one, to be taught something anyhow, anywhere—but no one took any pains with him, and he had no friends near who could help him.

At last one day, after some weary months had passed, Mr. Murdstone told him he was to go to London and earn his own living. There was a place for him at Murdstone & Grinby's, a firm in the wine trade. His lodging and clothes would be provided for him by his step-father, and he would earn enough for his food and pocket money. The next day David was sent up to London with the mana-ger, dressed in a shabby little white hat, with black crape round it for his mother, a black jacket, and hard, stiff corduroy trousers, a little fellow of ten years old to fight his own battles with the world!

His place, he found, was one of the lowest in the firm of

Murdstone & Grinby, with boys of no education and in quite an inferior station to himself—his duties were to wash the bottles, stick on labels, and so on.　David was utterly miserable at being degraded in this way, when he thought of his former companions, Steerforth and Traddles, and his hopes of becoming a learned and distinguished man, and shed bitter tears, as he feared he would forget all he had learnt at school.　His lodging, one bare little room, was in the house of some people named Micawber, shiftless, careless, good-natured people, who were always in debt and difficulties.　David felt great pity for their misfortunes and did what he could to help poor Mrs. Micawber to sell her books and other little things she could spare, to buy food for herself, her husband, and their four children.　David was too young and childish to know how to provide properly for himself, and often found he was obliged to live on bread and slices of cold pudding at the end of the week.　If he had not been a very innocent-minded, good little boy, he might easily have fallen into bad ways at this time.　But God took care of the orphan boy and kept him from harm.　The dear little unselfish fellow would not even tell Peggotty how miserable he was, for fear of distressing her.

The troubles of the Micawbers increased more and more until at last they were obliged to leave London.　David was very sad at this, for he had been with them so long that he felt they were his friends, and the prospect of being once more utterly alone, and having to find a lodging with strangers, made him so unhappy that he determined to endure this sort of life no longer.　The last Sunday the Micawbers were in town he dined with them. He had bought a spotted horse for their little boy, and a doll for the little girl, and had saved up a shilling for the poor servant maid.　After he had seen them off the next morning by the coach, he wrote to Peggotty to ask her if she knew where his aunt, Miss Betsey Trotwood, lived, and to borrow half-a-guinea ; for he had resolved to run away from Murdstone & Grinby's, and go to his aunt and tell her his story.　He remembered his mother telling him of her visit when he was a baby, and that she fancied

Miss Betsey had stroked her hair gently, and this gave him courage to appeal to her. Peggotty wrote, enclosing the half-guinea, and saying she only knew Miss Trotwood lived near Dover, but whether in that place itself, or at Folkestone, Sandgate, or Hythe, she could not tell. Hearing that all these places were close together, David made up his mind to start. As he had received his week's wages in advance, he waited till the following Saturday, thinking it would not be honest to go before. He went out to look for some one to carry his box to the coach office, and unfortunately employed a wicked young man who not only ran off with the box, but robbed him of his half-guinea, leaving poor David in dire distress. In despair, he started off to walk to Dover, and was forced to sell his waistcoat to buy some bread. The first night he found his way to his old school at Blackheath, and slept on a haystack close by, feeling some comfort in the thought of the boys being near. He knew Steerforth had left, or he would have tried to see him.

On he trudged the next day and sold his jacket at Chatham to a dreadful old man, who kept him waiting all day for the money, which was only one shilling and fourpence. He was afraid to buy anything but bread or to spend any money on a bed or a shelter for the night, and was terribly frightened by some rough tramps, who threw stones at him when he did not answer to their calls. After six days, he arrived at Dover, ragged, dusty, and half-dead with hunger and fatigue. But here, at first, he could get no tidings of his aunt, and, in despair, was going to try some of the other places Peggotty had mentioned, when the driver of a fly dropped his horsecloth, and as David was handing it up to him, he saw something kind in the man's face that encouraged him to ask once more if he knew where Miss Trotwood lived.

The man directed him towards some houses on the heights, and thither David toiled. Going into a little shop, he by chance met with Miss Trotwood's maid, who showed him the house, and went in leaving him standing at the gate, a forlorn little creature, without a jacket or waistcoat, his white hat crushed out of shape, his shoes worn out, his shirt and trousers torn and stained, his pretty curly hair tangled, his face and hands sunburnt, and covered with dust. Lifting his big, wistful eyes to one of the windows above, he saw a pleasant-faced gentleman with grey hair, who nodded at him several times, then shook his head and went away. David was just turning away to think what he should do, when a tall, erect, elderly lady, with a gardening apron on and a knife in her hand, came out of the house, and began to dig up a root in the garden.

"Go away," she said. "Go away. No boys here."

But David felt desperate. Going in softly, he stood beside her, and touched her with his finger, and said timidly, "If you please, ma'am——" and when she looked up, he went on—

"Please, aunt, I am your nephew."

"Oh, Lord!" she exclaimed in astonishment, and sat flat down on the path, staring at him, while he went on—

"I am David Copperfield of Blunderstone, in Suffolk, where you came the night I was born, and saw my dear mamma. I have been very unhappy since she died. I have been slighted and taught nothing, and thrown upon myself, and put to work not fit for me. It made me run away to you. I was robbed at first starting out and have walked all the way, and have never slept in a bed since I began the journey." Here he broke into a passion of crying, and his aunt jumped up and took him into the house, where she opened a cupboard and took out some bottles, pouring some of the contents of each into his mouth, not noticing in her agitation what they were, for David fancied he tasted aniseed

water, anchovy sauce, and salad dressing! Then
she put him upon the sofa and sent the servant to
ask "Mr. Dick" to come down. The gentleman
whom David had seen at the window came in
and was told by Miss Trotwood who the ragged
little object on the sofa was, and she finished
by saying—

"Now here you see young David Copperfield, and the question is, What shall I do with
him?"

"Do with him?" answered Mr. Dick.
Then, after some consideration, and looking
at David, he said, "Why, if I was you, I should
wash him!"

Miss Trotwood was quite pleased at this,
and a warm bath was got ready at once, after
which David was dressed in a shirt and trousers
belonging to Mr. Dick (for Janet had burned
his rags), rolled up in several shawls, and put
on the sofa till dinner-time, where he slept, and woke with the
impression that his aunt had come and put his hair off his face,
and murmured, "Pretty fellow, poor fellow."

After dinner he had to tell his story all over again to his
aunt and Mr. Dick. Miss Trotwood again asked Mr. Dick's
advice, and was delighted when that gentleman suggested he
should be put to bed. David knelt down to say his prayers that
night in a pleasant room facing the sea, and as he lay in the clean,
snow-white bed, he felt so grateful and comforted that he prayed
earnestly he might never be homeless again, and might never
forget the homeless.

The next morning his aunt told him she had written to Mr.
Murdstone. David was alarmed to think that his step-father
knew where he was, and exclaimed—

"Oh, I don't know what I shall do if I have to go back to
Mr. Murdstone!"

But his aunt said nothing of her intentions, and David was uncertain what was to become of him. He hoped she might befriend him.

At last Mr. and Miss Murdstone arrived. To Miss Betsey's great indignation, Miss Murdstone rode a donkey across the green in front of the house, and stopped at the gate. Nothing made Miss Trotwood so angry as to see donkeys on that green, and David had already seen several battles between his aunt or Janet and the donkey boys.

After driving away the donkey and the boy who had dared to bring it there, Miss Trotwood received her visitors. David she kept near her, fenced in with a chair.

Mr. Murdstone told Miss Betsey that David was a very bad, stubborn, violent-tempered boy, whom he had tried to improve, but could not succeed; that he had put him in a respectable business from which he had run away. If Miss Trotwood chose to protect and encourage him now, she must do it always, for he had come to fetch him away there and then, and if he was not ready to come, and Miss Trotwood did not wish to give him up to be dealt with exactly as Mr. Murdstone liked, he would cast him off for always, and have no more to do with him.

"Are you ready to go, David?" asked his aunt.

But David answered no, and begged and prayed her for his father's sake to befriend and protect him, for neither Mr. nor Miss Murdstone had ever liked him or been kind to him, and had made his mamma, who always loved him dearly, very unhappy about him, and he had been very miserable.

"Mr. Dick," said Miss Trotwood, "what shall I do with this child?"

Mr. Dick considered. "Have him measured for a suit of clothes directly."

"Mr. Dick," said Miss Trotwood, "your common sense is invaluable."

Then she pulled David towards her, and said to Mr. Murdstone, "You can go when you like. I'll take my chance with the boy. If he's all you say he is I can at least do as much for him as you have done. But I don't believe a word of it."

Then she told Mr. Murdstone what she thought of the way he had treated David and his mother, which did not make that gentleman feel very comfortable, and finished by turning to Miss Murdstone, and saying : " Good-day to you, too, ma'am, and if I ever see you ride a donkey across my green again, as sure as you have a head upon your shoulders, I'll knock your bonnet off and tread upon it ! "

This startled Miss Murdstone so much that she went off quite quietly with her brother, while David, overjoyed, threw his arms round his aunt's neck, and kissed and thanked her with great heartiness.

Some clothes were bought for him and marked " Trotwood Copperfield," for his aunt wished to call him by her name.

Now David felt his troubles were over, and he began quite a new life, well cared for and kindly treated. He was sent to a very nice school in Canterbury, where his aunt left him with these words, which David never forgot :

" Trot, be a credit to yourself, to me, and Mr. Dick, and Heaven be with you. Never be mean in anything, never be false, never be cruel. Avoid these three vices, Trot, and I shall always be hopeful of you."

David did his best to show his gratitude to his dear aunt by studying hard, and trying to be all she could wish.

When you are older you can read how he grew up to be a good, clever man, and met again all his old friends, and made many new ones.

M

OLIVER TWIST

ONCE upon a time there was born in a country workhouse a baby boy. He was a poor, weakly little child, and at the time of his birth his mother died, and nobody knew who she was, and nobody had heard of his father or any of his relations, so he was just a poor little atom in this wide, wide world of ours.

The workhouse people called him Oliver Twist, and brought him up with a lot of other miserable children who were also without fathers or mothers. The poor boy was beaten and half-starved, and was altogether as unhappy as unhappy can be, for workhouses were different in those days to what they are now.

The room in which the boys were fed was a large stone hall, with a copper at one end, out of which the master, dressed in an apron for the purpose, and assisted by one or two women, ladled the gruel at meal-times. Of this festive composition each boy had one porringer, and no more—except on occasions of great public rejoicing, when he had two ounces and a quarter of bread besides. The bowls never wanted washing. The boys polished them with their spoons till they shone again ; and, when they had performed this operation (which never took very long, the spoons being nearly as large as the bowls), they would sit staring at the copper with such eager eyes as if they could have devoured the very bricks of which it was composed, employing themselves meanwhile in sucking their fingers most assiduously, with the view of catching up any stray splashes of gruel that might have been cast thereon. Boys have generally excellent appetites, and Oliver Twist and his companions suffered the tortures of slow starvation for several months ; but at last they got so voracious and wild with hunger that one boy, who was tall for his age, and hadn't been used to that sort of thing (for his father had kept a small cookshop), hinted darkly to his companions that unless he had another basin of gruel *per diem* he was afraid he might some night happen to eat the boy who slept next him, who happened to be a weakly youth of tender age. He had a wild, hungry eye, and they implicitly believed him. A council was held ; lots were cast who should walk up to the master after supper that evening, and ask for more, and it fell to Oliver Twist.

The evening arrived. The boys took their places. The master, in his cook's uniform, stationed himself at the copper, his pauper assistants ranged themselves behind him, the gruel was served out, and a long grace was said over the short commons. The gruel disappeared. The boys whispered to each other and winked at Oliver, while his next neighbours nudged him. Child as he was, he was desperate with hunger and reckless with misery. He rose from the table, and advancing to the master, basin and spoon in hand, said, somewhat alarmed at his own temerity :

" Please, sir, I want some more."

The master was a fat healthy man ; but he turned very pale. He gazed in stupefied astonishment on the small rebel for some seconds, and then clung for support to the copper. The assistants were paralysed with wonder, the boys with fear.

"What!" said the master at length, in a faint voice.

"Please, sir," replied Oliver, "I want some more."

The master aimed a blow at Oliver's head with the ladle, pinioned him in his arms, and shrieked aloud for the Beadle.

The board was sitting in solemn conclave, when Mr. Bumble, the Beadle, rushed into the room in great excitement, and addressing the gentleman in the high chair, said :

"Mr. Limbkins, I beg your pardon, sir ! Oliver Twist has asked for more !"

There was a general start. Horror was depicted on every countenance.

"For *more !*" said Mr. Limbkins. "Compose yourself, Bumble, and answer me distinctly. Do I understand that he asked for more after he had eaten the supper allotted by the dietary ? "

"He did, sir," replied Bumble.

"That boy will be hung," said a gentleman in a white waistcoat. "I know that boy will be hung."

Nobody controverted the prophetic gentleman's opinion. An animated discussion took place. Oliver was ordered into instant confinement, and a bill was next morning pasted on the outside of the gate offering a reward of five pounds to anybody who would take Oliver Twist off the hands of the parish. In other words, five pounds and Oliver Twist were offered to any man or woman who wanted an apprentice to any trade, business or calling.

Well, the bill on the gate had its effect, and Oliver, at the early age of ten, left the workhouse to earn his living. He was apprenticed to an undertaker called Mr. Sowerberry, and here he was as badly treated as he had been at the workhouse. Mr. Sowerberry had another apprentice, named Noah Claypole, who was a horrid, disagreeable boy. He and the servant, Charlotte, were continually bullying poor little Oliver.

One day Noah went too far ; he abused Oliver's mother.

" Work'us," said Noah—he always called Oliver " Work'us " —" how's your mother ? "

" She's dead," replied Oliver. " Don't you say anything about her to me ! "

Oliver's colour rose as he said this, he breathed quickly, and there was a curious working of the mouth and nostrils, which Mr. Claypole thought must be the immediate precursor of a violent fit of crying. Under this impression he returned to the charge.

" What did she die of, Work'us ? " said Noah.

" Of a broken heart some of our old nurses told me," replied Oliver, more as if he were talking to himself than answering Noah. " I think I know what it must be to die of that ! "

" Tol de rol lol lol, right fol lairy, Work'us," said Noah, as a tear rolled down Oliver's cheek. " What's set you a-snivelling now ? "

" Not *you*," replied Oliver, hastily brushing the tear away. " Don't think it."

" Oh, not me, eh ? " sneered Noah.

" No, not you," replied Oliver sharply. " There that's enough. Don't say anything more to me about her ; you'd better not ! "

" Better not ! " exclaimed Noah. " Well ! Better not ! Work'us, don't be impudent. *Your* mother, too ! She was a nice 'un, she was. Oh, Lor ! " And here Noah nodded his head expressively, and curled up as much of his small red nose as muscular action could collect together for the occasion.

"Yer know, Work'us," continued Noah, emboldened by Oliver's silence, and speaking in a jeering tone of affected pity— of all tones the most annoying—"yer know, Work'us, it can't be helped now, and of course yer couldn't help it then, and I'm very sorry for it, and I'm sure we all are, and pity yer very much. But yer must know, Work'us, yer mother was a regular right-down bad 'un."

"What did you say?" inquired Oliver, looking up very quickly.

"A right-down bad 'un, Work'us," replied Noah, coolly. "And it's a great deal better, Work'us, that she died when she did, or else she'd have been hard labouring in Bridewell, or transported, or hung, which is more likely than either, isn't it?"

Crimson with fury, Oliver started up, overthrew the chair and table, seized Noah by the throat, shook him in the violence of his rage till his teeth chattered in his head, and, collecting his whole force into one heavy blow, felled him to the ground.

A minute ago the boy had looked the quiet, mild, dejected creature that harsh treatment had made him. But his spirit was roused at last; the cruel insult to his dead mother had set his blood on fire. His breast heaved; his attitude was erect; his eye bright and vivid; his whole person changed, as he stood glaring over the cowardly tormentor who now lay crouching at his feet, and defied him with an energy he had never known before.

"He'll murder me!" blubbered Noah. "Charlotte! Missis! Here's the new boy a-murdering of me! Help! help! Oliver's gone mad! Charlotte!"

Noah's shouts were responded to by a loud scream from Charlotte and a louder from Mrs. Sowerberry, the former of whom rushed into the kitchen by a side-door, while the latter paused on the staircase till she was quite certain that it was consistent with the preservation of human life to come further down.

"Oh, you little wretch!" screamed Charlotte, seizing Oliver with her utmost force, which was about equal to that of a moderately strong man in particularly good training. "Oh, you little un-grate-ful, mur-de-rous, hor-rid villain!" And between every syllable Charlotte gave Oliver a blow with all her might, accompanying it with a scream for the benefit of society.

Charlotte's fist was by no means a light one; but, lest it should not be effectual in calming Oliver's wrath, Mrs. Sowerberry plunged into the kitchen and assisted to hold him with one hand while she scratched his face with the other. In this favourable position of affairs Noah rose from the ground and pommelled him behind.

This was rather too violent exercise to last long. When they were all three wearied out and could tear and beat no longer, they dragged Oliver, struggling and shouting, but nothing daunted, into the dust-cellar, and there locked him up. This being done, Mrs. Sowerberry sank into a chair and burst into tears.

"Bless her, she's going off!" said Charlotte. "A glass of water, Noah dear. Make haste!"

"Oh! Charlotte," said Mrs. Sowerberry, speaking as well as she could through a deficiency of breath and a sufficiency of cold water, which Noah had poured over her head and shoulders. "Oh! Charlotte, what a mercy we have not all been murdered in our beds!"

"Ah! mercy indeed, ma'am," was the reply. "I only hope this'll teach master not to have any more of these dreadful creatures that are born to be murderers and robbers from their very cradle. Poor Noah! He was all but killed, ma'am, when I come in."

"Poor fellow!" said Mrs. Sowerberry, looking pityingly on the charity-boy.

Noah, whose top waistcoat-button might have been somewhere on a level with the crown of Oliver's head, rubbed his eyes with the inside of his wrists while this commiseration was bestowed upon him, and performed some affecting tears and sniffs.

"What's to be done?" exclaimed Mrs. Sowerberry. "Your master's not at home, there's not a man in the house, and he'll kick that door down in ten minutes." Oliver's vigorous plunges against the bit of timber in question rendered this occurrence highly probable.

"Dear, dear! I don't know, ma'am," said Charlotte, "unless we send for the police officers."

"Or the millingtary," suggested Mr. Claypole.

"No, no," said Mrs. Sowerberry, bethinking herself of the Beadle. "Run to Mr. Bumble, Noah, and tell him to come here directly, and not to lose a minute; never mind your cap! Make haste! You can hold a knife to that black eye as you run along. It'll keep the swelling down."

Noah did not stop to reply, but started off at his fullest speed; and very much it astonished the people who were out walking to see a charity-boy tearing through the streets pell-mell, with no cap on his head and a clasp-knife at his eye.

Poor Oliver was terribly punished for this, so much so that he determined to run away; but it was not until he was left alone in the silence and stillness of the gloomy workshop of the under-taker that Oliver gave way to the feelings which the day's treatment may be supposed likely to have awakened in a mere child. He had listened to their taunts with a look of contempt; he had borne the lash without a cry, for he felt that pride swelling in his heart which would have kept down a shriek to the last, though they had roasted him alive. But now, when there was none to see or hear him, he fell upon his knees on the floor, and, hiding his face in his hands, wept such tears as, God send for the credit of our nature, few so young may ever have cause to pour out before Him!

For a long time Oliver remained motionless in this attitude. The candle was burning low in the socket when he rose to his feet. Having gazed cautiously round him and listened

intently, he gently undid the fastenings of the door and looked abroad.

It was a cold, dark night. The stars seemed to the boy's eyes farther from the earth than he had ever seen them before ;

N

there was no wind, and the sombre shadows thrown by the trees upon the ground looked sepulchral and deathlike from being so still. He softly reclosed the door. Having availed himself of the expiring light of the candle to tie up in a handkerchief the few articles of wearing apparel he had, he sat himself down upon a bench to wait for morning.

With the first ray of light that struggled through the crevices in the shutters Oliver arose, and again unbarred the door. One timid look around, one moment's pause of hesitation; he had closed it behind him, and was in the open street.

He looked to the right and to the left, uncertain whither to fly. He remembered to have seen the waggons as they went out toiling up the hill. He took the same route, and, arriving at a footpath across the fields, which he knew, after some distance, led out again into the road, struck into it, and walked quickly on.

Along this same footpath Oliver well remembered he had trotted beside Mr. Bumble, the Beadle. His heart beat quickly when he bethought himself of this, and he half resolved to turn back. He had come a long way, though, and should lose a great deal of time by doing so. Besides, it was so early that there was very little fear of his being seen, so he walked on.

He reached a house. There was no appearance of its inmates stirring at that early hour. Oliver stopped and peeped into the garden. A child was weeding one of the little beds; as he stopped, he raised his pale face and disclosed the features of one of his former companions. Oliver felt glad to see him before he went, for, though younger than himself, he had been his little friend and playmate. They had been beaten and starved and shut up together many and many a time.

"Hush, Dick!" said Oliver, as the boy ran to the gate and thrust his thin arm between the rails to greet him. "Is anyone up?"

"Nobody but me," replied the child.

"You mustn't say you saw me, Dick," said Oliver. "I am running away. They beat and ill-use me, Dick, and I am going

OLIVER TWIST ASKS FOR MORE

to seek my fortune some long way off. I don't know where. How pale you are!"

"I heard the doctor tell them I was dying," replied the child with a faint smile. "I am very glad to see you, dear; but don't stop, don't stop!"

"Yes, yes, I will, to say good-bye to you," replied Oliver. "I shall see you again, Dick. I know I shall! You will be well and happy!"

"I hope so," replied the child. "After I am dead, but not before. I know the doctor must be right, Oliver, because I dream so much of heaven and angels and kind faces that I never see when I am awake. Kiss me," said the child, climbing up the low gate and flinging his little arms round Oliver's neck. "Good-bye, dear! God bless you!"

The blessing was from a young child's lips, but it was the first that Oliver had ever heard invoked upon his head, and through the struggles and sufferings and troubles and changes of his after life he never once forgot it.

So this poor, friendless boy trudged off to London. He had no idea what he was going to do, where he was going to sleep, or when he would have his next meal; all he wanted was to get away from the cruel, unhappy life he had been leading.

Unfortunately, Oliver was to suffer worse miseries. For seven weary days he begged his way, sleeping under haystacks and such-like places, and was nearly dying of starvation and hunger when he met a strange boy. This boy, who was some years older than Oliver, gave him something to eat, and then took him to his home.

It was an awful home this, where the boy took Oliver, and awful people lived in it—horrible, wicked people, who lived entirely by stealing. Oliver was an innocent lad, and did not discover for some time that he was living with thieves; but one day he was out with the boy who had taken him home and another boy, when they saw an old gentleman standing by a bookstall. Immediately the two boys who were with Oliver walked stealthily across the road and slunk close behind the old gentleman. Oliver walked a few paces after them, and not knowing whether to advance or retire, stood looking on in silent amazement.

The old gentleman was a very respectable-looking personage, with a powdered head and gold spectacles. He was dressed in a bottle-green coat with a black velvet collar, wore white trousers, and carried a smart bamboo cane under his arm. He had taken up a book from the stall ; and there he stood reading away as hard as if he were in his elbow-chair in his own study. It is very possible that he fancied himself there indeed, for it was plain, from his utter abstraction, that he saw not the bookstall, nor the street, nor the boys, nor, in short, anything but the book itself, which he was reading straight through, turning over the leaf when he got to the bottom of a page, beginning at the top line of the next one and going regularly on with the greatest interest and eagerness.

What was Oliver's horror and alarm, as he stood a few paces off, looking on with his eyelids as wide open as they would possibly go, to see one of the boys plunge his hand into the old gentleman's pocket, and draw from thence a handkerchief ! To see him hand the same to the other boy, and finally to behold them both running away round the corner at full speed !

Oliver stood for a moment with the blood so tingling through all his veins from terror that he felt as if he were in a burning fire, then, confused and frightened, he took to his heels, and not knowing what he did, made off as fast as he could lay his feet to the ground.

This was all done in a minute's space. In the very instant when Oliver began to run, the old gentleman, putting his hand to his pocket and missing his handkerchief, turned sharp round. Seeing the boy scudding away at such a rapid pace he very naturally concluded him to be the depredator, and, shouting "Stop thief!" with all his might, made off after him, book in hand.

But the old gentleman was not the only person who raised the hue and cry. The two young thieves, unwilling to attract public attention by running down the open street, had merely retired into the very first door-way round the corner. They no sooner heard the cry and saw Oliver running than, guessing exactly how the matter stood, they issued forth with great promptitude, and, shouting "Stop thief!" too, joined in the pursuit like good citizens.

Although Oliver had been brought up by philosophers he was not theoretically acquainted with the beautiful axiom that self-preservation is the first law of nature. If he had been, perhaps he would have been prepared for this. Not being prepared, however, it alarmed him the more; so away he went like the wind, with the old gentleman and the two boys roaring and shouting behind him.

"Stop thief! Stop thief!" There is a magic in the sound. The tradesman leaves his counter and the carman his waggon, the butcher throws down his tray, the baker his basket, the milk-man his pail, the errand-boy his parcels, the schoolboy his marbles, the pavior his pickaxe, the child his battledore. Away they run, pell-mell, helter-skelter, slap-dash, tearing, yelling and screaming, knocking down the passengers as they turn the corners, rousing up the dogs and astonishing the fowls ; and streets, squares and courts re-echo with the sound.

"Stop thief! Stop thief!" The cry is taken up by a hundred voices, and the crowd accumulates at every turning. Away they fly, splashing through the mud and rattling along the pavements ; up go the windows, out run the people, onward tears the mob, a whole audience desert Punch in the very thickest of the plot, and joining the rushing throng swell the shout, and lend fresh vigour to the cry—

"Stop thief! Stop thief!"

"Stop thief! Stop thief!" There is a passion *for hunting something* deeply implanted in the human breast. One wretched, breathless child, panting with exhaustion, terror in his looks, agony in his eyes, large drops of perspiration streaming down his face, strains every nerve to make head upon his pursuers, and as they follow on his track and gain upon him every instant they hail his decreasing strength with still louder shouts, and whoop and scream with joy, "Stop thief!"

Stopped at last! A clever blow! He is down upon the pavement, and the crowd eagerly gathers round him, each new-comer jostling and struggling with the others to catch a glimpse. "Stand aside!" "Give him a little air!" "Nonsense, he don't deserve it!" "Where's the gentleman?" "Here he is, coming down the street." "Make room there for the gentleman!" "Is this the boy, sir?" "Yes."

Oliver lay, covered with mud and dust, and bleeding from the mouth, looking wildly round upon the heap of faces that surrounded him, when the old gentleman was officiously dragged and pushed into the circle by the foremost of the pursuers.

"Yes," said the gentleman, "I am afraid it is the boy."

"Afraid!" murmured the crowd. "That's a good 'un."

"Poor fellow!" said the gentleman ; "he has hurt himself."

"*I* did that, sir," said a great lubberly fellow, stepping forward ; "and preciously *I* cut my knuckle agin' his mouth. *I* stopped him, sir."

The fellow touched his hat with a grin, expecting something for his pains; but the old gentleman, eyeing him with an expression of dislike, looked anxiously round as if he contemplated running away himself, which it is very possible he might have attempted to do, and thus afforded another chase, had not a police-officer (who is generally the last person to arrive in such cases) at that moment made his way through the crowd, and seized Oliver by the collar.

"Come, get up!" said the man roughly.

"It wasn't me, indeed, sir! Indeed, indeed, it was two other boys," said Oliver, clasping his hands passionately, and looking round. "They are here somewhere."

"Oh, no, they ain't," said the officer. He meant this to be ironical, but it was true besides, for the real thieves had filed off down the first convenient court they came to. "Come, get up!"

"Don't hurt him," said the old gentleman compassionately.

"Oh, no, I won't hurt him," replied the officer, tearing his jacket half off his back in proof thereof. "Come, I know you; it won't do. Will you stand upon your legs?"

Oliver, who could hardly stand, made a shift to raise himself on his feet, and was at once lugged along the streets by the jacket-collar at a rapid pace. The gentleman walked on with them by the officer's side, and as many of the crowd as could achieve the feat got a little ahead and stared back at Oliver from time to time. The boys shouted in triumph, and on they went.

Poor Oliver was taken before a magistrate, and was tried and sentenced to go to prison for three months; and the police were taking the boy away when an elderly man of decent but poor appearance, clad in an old suit of black, rushed hastily into the office, and advanced towards the magistrate.

"Stop! stop! Don't take him away! For heaven's sake, stop a moment!" cried the new-comer, breathless with haste.

"I saw three boys," continued the man, "two others and the prisoner here, loitering on the opposite side of the way when this gentleman was reading. The robbery was committed by another boy. I saw it done, and I saw that this boy was perfectly amazed and stupefied by it." Having by this time recovered a little breath, the worthy bookstall-keeper proceeded to relate, in a more coherent manner, the exact circumstances of the robbery.

So it happened that Oliver did not go to prison, but instead was taken home by the old gentleman who had been robbed, and was tenderly cared for. Indeed, Oliver was happy for the first time in his life.

It would be very nice to be able to tell you that Oliver stayed with this kind old gentleman; but, alas! it was not so. Those wicked thieves stole Oliver away, and took him back to their awful home, and threatened to kill him if he ran away again.

Among these thieves there was one more desperate and wicked than the others. His name was Bill Sikes. Well, one night Sikes and another man went out to rob a house, and took Oliver with them to help, poor boy!

When they came to the house, which was in the country, Sikes, who was in the garden, put Oliver quietly through a little window, and told him to go and open the street door and let them in.

"Take this lantern," said Sikes. "You see the stairs afore you?"

Oliver, more dead than alive, gasped out, "Yes." Sikes, pointing to the street door with the pistol-barrel, briefly advised him to take notice that he was well within shot all the way, and that if he faltered he would fall dead that instant.

"It's done in a minute," said Sikes, in the same low whisper. "Directly I leave go of you do your work. Hark!"

"What's that?" whispered the other man.

They listened intently.

"Nothing," said Sikes, releasing his hold of Oliver. "Now!"

In the short time he had had to collect his senses the boy had firmly resolved that, whether he died in the attempt or not, he would make one effort to dart upstairs from the hall and alarm the family.

Filled with this idea he advanced at once, but stealthily.

"Come back!" suddenly cried Sikes aloud. "Back! back!"

Scared by the sudden breaking of the dead stillness of the place, and by a loud cry which followed it, Oliver let his lantern fall, and knew not whether to advance or fly.

The cry was repeated—a light appeared—a vision of two terrified half-dressed men at the top of the stairs swam

before his eyes—a flash—a loud noise—a smoke—a crash somewhere, but where he knew not—and he staggered back.

Sikes muttered horribly to himself, grinding his teeth with rage, as he hurried along. Then for a moment he rested the body of the wounded boy across his bended knee, and turned his head for an instant to look back at his pursuers.

There was little to be made out in the mist and darkness; but the loud shouting of men vibrated through the air, and the barking of the neighbouring dogs, roused by the sound of the alarm-bell, resounded in every direction.

"Stop, you hound!" cried the robber, shouting after the other burglar, Toby Crackit, who, making the best use of his long legs, was already ahead—"Stop!"

O

The repetition of the word brought Toby to a dead standstill, for he was not quite satisfied that he was beyond the range of pistol-shot, and Sikes was in no mood to be played with.

"Bear a hand with the boy," roared Sikes, beckoning furiously to his confederate. "Come back!"

Toby made a show of returning, but ventured in a low voice, broken for want of breath to intimate considerable reluctance as he came slowly along.

"Quicker!" cried Sikes, laying the boy in a dry ditch at his feet, and drawing a pistol from his pocket. "Don't play the booby with me."

At this moment the noise grew louder, and Sikes again looking round could discern that the men who had given chase were already climbing the gate of the field in which he stood, and that a couple of dogs were some paces in advance of them.

"It's all up, Bill," cried Toby; "drop the kid and show 'em your heels."

With this parting advice Mr. Crackit, preferring the chance of being shot by his friend to the certainty of being taken by his enemies, fairly turned tail, and darted off at full speed.

Sikes clenched his teeth, took one look round, threw over the prostrate form of Oliver the cape in which he had been hurriedly muffled, ran along the front of the hedge as if to distract the attention of those behind from the spot where the boy lay, paused for a second before another hedge which met it at right angles, and whirling his pistol high into the air, cleared it at a bound, and was gone.

"Ho, ho, there!" cried a tremulous voice in the rear. "Pincher, Neptune, come here, come here!"

The dogs, which in common with their masters seemed to have no particular relish for the sport in which they were engaged, readily answered to this command, and three men, who had by this time advanced some distance into the field, stopped to take counsel together.

The result of their talk was that they returned to their home without finding poor Oliver. As a matter of fact, they were all very nervous, for it's by no means a pleasant thing to have to turn out of a warm bed on a cold night to hunt armed burglars—desperate, wicked men who would not hesitate to shoot you.

* * * * *

The air grew colder as day came slowly on, and the mist rolled along the ground like a dense cloud of smoke; the grass was wet, the pathways and low places were all mire and water, and the damp breath of an unwholesome wind went languidly by with a hollow moaning. Still Oliver lay motionless and insensible on the spot where Sikes had left him.

Morning drew on apace; the air became more sharp and piercing as its first dull hue—the death of night rather than the birth of day—glimmered faintly in the sky. The objects which had looked dim and terrible in the darkness grew more and more defined, and gradually resolved into their familiar shapes. The rain came down thick and fast, and pattered noisily among the leafless bushes. But Oliver felt it not as it beat against him, for he still lay stretched, helpless and unconscious, on his bed of clay.

At length a low cry of pain broke the stillness that prevailed, and, uttering it, the boy awoke. His left arm, rudely bandaged in a shawl, hung heavy and useless at his side, and the bandage was saturated with blood.

He was so weak that he could scarcely raise himself into a sitting posture, and when he had done so, he looked feebly round for help, and groaned with pain. Trembling in every joint from cold and exhaustion, he made an effort to stand upright, but shuddering from head to foot, fell prostrate on the ground.

After a short return of the stupor in which he had been so long plunged, Oliver, urged by a creeping sickness at his heart, which seemed to warn him that if he lay there he must surely die, got upon his feet and essayed to walk.

His head was dizzy, and he staggered to and fro like a drunken man; but he kept up nevertheless, and, with his head drooping languidly on his breast, went stumbling onward he knew not whither.

And now hosts of bewildering and confused ideas came crowding on his mind. He seemed to be still walking between Sikes and Crackit, who were angrily disputing, for the very words they said sounded in his ears; and when he caught his own attention, as it were, by making some violent effort to save himself from falling, he found that he was talking to them.

Then he was alone with Sikes, plodding on as they had done the previous day, and as shadowy people passed them by, he felt the robber's grasp upon his wrist. Suddenly he started back at the report of firearms, and there rose into the air loud cries and shouts; lights gleamed before his eyes, and all was noise and tumult as some unseen hand bore him hurriedly away. Through all these rapid visions there ran an undefined, uneasy consciousness of pain, which wearied and tormented him incessantly.

Thus he staggered on, creeping almost mechanically between the bars of gates or through hedge-gaps as they came in his way, until he reached a road; and here the rain began to fall so heavily that it roused him.

He looked about, and saw that at no great distance there was a house, which perhaps he could reach. Seeing his condition they might have compassion on him, and if they did not it would be better, he thought, to die near human beings than in the lonely open fields.

He summoned up all his strength for one last trial, and bent his faltering steps towards it.

As he drew nearer to this house a feeling came over him that he had seen it before. He remembered nothing of its details, but the shape and aspect of the building seemed familiar to him.

That garden wall! On the grass inside he had fallen on his knees last night and prayed the two men's mercy. It was the very same house they had attempted to rob. Oliver felt such fear come over him when he recognised the place, that for the instant he forgot the agony of his wound, and thought only of flight!

Flight! He could scarcely stand; and if he were in full possession of all the best powers of his slight and youthful frame, where could he fly to? He pushed against the garden gate; it was unlocked, and swung open on its hinges.

He tottered across the lawn, climbed the steps, and knocked faintly at the door, and his whole strength failing him, sank down against one of the pillars of the little portico.

    *   *   *   *   *   *

And now what happened to this poor wretched little boy?

The door was opened, and he was recognised as one of the daring burglars. He was seized and dragged into the house by the man-servant, and a doctor was sent for.

Doctor Losberne was one of the kindest men in the world, and he had Oliver put to bed, and dressed his wound and did everything he could for him. Then afterwards he saw Mrs. Maylie, the lady of the house, and her daughter Rose, to tell them about the dreadful burglar that had broken into the house the night before.

"This is a very extraordinary thing, Mrs. Maylie," said the doctor, standing with his back to the door as if to keep it shut.

"He is not in danger, I hope?" said the old lady.

"Why, that would not be an extraordinary thing, under the circumstances," replied the doctor, "though I don't think he is. Have you seen this thief?"

"No," rejoined the old lady.

"Nor heard anything about him?"

"No. Rose wished to see the man," said Mrs. Maylie, "but I wouldn't hear of it."

"Humph!" rejoined the doctor. "There's nothing very alarming in his appearance. Have you any objection to see him in my presence?"

"If it be necessary," replied the old lady, "certainly not."

"Then I think it is necessary," said the doctor; "at all events, I am quite sure that you would deeply regret not having done so if you postponed it. He is perfectly quiet and comfortable now. Allow me—Miss Rose, will you permit me? Not the slightest fear, I pledge you my honour."

With many more loquacious assurances that they would be agreeably surprised in the aspect of the criminal, the doctor drew the young lady's arm through one of his, and offering his disengaged hand to Mrs. Maylie, led them with much ceremony and stateliness upstairs.

"Now," said the doctor in a whisper, as he softly turned the handle of a bedroom door, "let us hear what you think of him. He has not been shaved very recently, but he doesn't look at all ferocious, notwithstanding. Stop, though—let me see that he is in visiting order first."

Stepping before them he looked into the room, and,

motioning them to advance, closed the door when they had entered, and gently drew back the curtains of the bed.

Upon it, instead of the dogged, black-visaged ruffian they had expected to behold, there lay a mere child, worn with pain and exhaustion, and sunk into a deep sleep.

His wounded arm, bound and splintered up, was crossed upon his breast, and his head reclined upon the other, which was half hidden by his long hair as it streamed over the pillow.

The honest gentleman held the curtain in his hand, and looked on for a minute or so in silence. Whilst he was watching the patient thus, the younger lady glided softly past, and seating herself in a chair by the bedside, gathered Oliver's hair from his face, and as she stooped over him her tears fell upon his forehead.

The boy stirred, and smiled in his sleep, as though these marks of pity and compassion had awakened some pleasant dream of a love and affection he had never known. Thus a strain of gentle music, or the rippling of water in a silent place, or the odour of a flower, or the mention of a familiar word, will sometimes call up sudden dim remembrances of scenes that never were in this life, which vanish like a breath, and which some brief memory of a happier existence, long gone by, would seem to have awakened, for no power of the human mind can ever recall them.

When Oliver awoke he told them all his strange history, but was often compelled to stop by pain and want of strength.

It was a solemn thing to hear, in the darkened room, the feeble voice of the sick child recounting a weary catalogue of evils and calamities which hard men had brought upon him.

Oliver's pillow was smoothed by women's hands that night, and loveliness and virtue watched him as he slept.

And this, let me tell you, was the end of the poor boy's troubles. It is a very strange thing to have to relate, but the pretty Rose Maylie turned out to be Oliver's aunt—his mother's own sister! From the moment he entered Mrs. Maylie's house his life was as happy as it had been miserable in the past. From that day forth he heard little more of that fearful place where the thieves lived, and the thieves themselves were caught and sent to prison, and thus came to the punishment they so richly deserved.